THE BIG BET

Bullseye

Owen B. Greenwald

EPIC
Press

Bullseye
The Big Bet: Book #3

Written by Owen B. Greenwald

Copyright © 2016 by Abdo Consulting Group, Inc.

Published by EPIC Press™
PO Box 398166
Minneapolis, MN 55439

Cover design by Candice Keimig
Images for cover art obtained from iStockPhoto.com
Edited by Ryan Hume

LIBRARY OF CONGRESS CATALOGING-IN-PUBLICATION DATA

Greenwald, Owen B.
Bullseye / Owen B. Greenwald.
p. cm. — (The big bet ; #3)
Summary: The Mafia's first mistake was not making sure Jason Jorgensen was dead.
Now the CPC is engaged in a covert war against the Mafia's operations—while
slowly, Jason and his team of con artists are whittling away at their senior members.
ISBN 978-1-68076-185-6 (hardcover)
1. Swindlers and swindling—Fiction. 2. Deception—Fiction. 3. Young adult
fiction. I. Title.
[Fic]—dc23
2015949055

EPICPRESS.COM

For Liz,
my fellow writer
whose horse-related expertise
was immensely helpful.

And for Paul Kivelson,
my almost-coauthor
who nonetheless got me invested
and helped shape the arc of the plot.
This series would not be what it was without you.

ONE

NE THING ABOUT NEW YORK CITY IS, IT'S FULL of hidden treasures. Take Meltkraft, for example. It's a great sandwich shop on MacDougal Street. It's small, but not *cramped*—just tight enough to give a sense of closeness and intimacy with your tablemates. The staff's friendly and helpful, and (of course) the sandwiches themselves are divine. Meltkraft doesn't stand out to tourists, but among New York's student population, it's the worst-kept secret in town. Guys like me are commonly seen in front of Meltkraft's awning—late teens, still carrying his backpack, compulsively checking his phone to see where his friends are. That's just part of a normal New York afternoon.

Of course, *my* situation—like me—was anything but normal. For one, I knew *exactly* where my friends were. Addie was approximately thirty feet to my left, wearing a business pantsuit and shades, and somehow managing to look almost twice her age. I was very deliberately not looking her way in case someone noticed and deduced we knew each other—and because I might have trouble looking away. Kira was several hundred yards down the street in her car, carefully watching Meltkraft's occupants with a telescope through their big shopfront window—assuming she was doing her job. Z was with Kira, relaying information for her. Whenever Kira wanted me to know something, she'd say it out loud and Z'd text it to me. That way, she never had to take her eye off the telescope.

For another, I wasn't actually here for a sandwich. My job was to stand here, a glorified cue-light for Addie. When Z gave me the go-ahead, I'd mutter, "Son-of-a-bitch said he'd be here a fucking hour ago!" loud enough for her to hear, and she'd make her move. I *would* be getting a sandwich later—ten minutes later, to be exact, when Z showed up pretending to be my late friend—but that was just to keep up appearances. It wasn't the outing's primary purpose, just a happy bonus.

Finally, I'm far more devilishly handsome than your average Meltkraft patron/high school student/New Yorker. That's probably the most important difference of all.

Normally, I wouldn't need four people for a relatively simple faux-collision, but extreme caution was the name of the game—had been since Las Vegas, where the Mafia'd tried to kill us. As far as they were concerned, they'd succeeded, and I didn't want them having any cause to suspect otherwise.

The collection of families known as the Mafia was a vast and complex organism, and the first order of business had been researching which family'd decided to bump us off. There was no reason to target the Gambinos if the Columbos were at fault, for example. The families worked together on occasion, but crime's a competitive business, and they were just as often at odds.

Furthermore, different families were active in different cities. This could've ended our revenge before it'd even started (if, say, the family from Vegas wasn't a New York family), but as it turned out, the five New York families maintain a presence in Las Vegas alongside the native families. And surprise, surprise, the family that'd hired us was native to New York—the Bonannos. They were practically right in our backyard.

We couldn't both convincingly fake our deaths and continue our lives as normal. I'd thought about it the whole flight home, and decided it was impossible. If four high schoolers vanished during a vacation in Las Vegas, it'd make *at least* local news—and it hadn't, as five seconds and a search engine would tell anyone who cared to look. And when the mob'd hired us, they'd sent a guy right to our school. He'd known our *names*. The moment they even *suspected* we'd dodged the grave, that was game over. Insert coin.

And with *that* in mind, you might conclude that it'd be safest to forget about the Bonanno family entirely, and not, for example, to set about identifying their members. Certainly not to shadow said members until you learned which restaurant was their traditional choice for lunch. And by loitering outside that restaurant with the intent of getting those members arrested, we'd given up all pretenses of *safety*. Revenge is rarely a safe process.

I can respect prioritizing safety from a philosophical standpoint, but I can't live that way myself. The mob'd hired us, then tried to kill us instead of paying up. Worse, they'd almost *succeeded*. I don't think anyone could experience that and not at least *entertain* the possibility of revenge, whatever the risk. And sure, our revenge *could* have been smaller-scale than *destroy or defang the entire Bonanno family,* but the Club for Perfect Cleanliness'd always been about dreaming big. And this time, it was personal.

That's a little more "cheesy movie poster tagline" than I meant it to sound, but it's still true. For the first time in CPC history, we weren't after a profit—we were just *mad*.

We all knew the risks. But despite—and maybe, in Kira's case, *because* of—that, we were committed. For my part, I was confident. The mob had only outmatched me in Vegas because I hadn't expected them. Now that they were a known entity, I was sure I could handle them. So far, I'd been right.

It'd been three weeks since the standoff in the desert, since that stumbling, endless walk back to civilization through the heavy night—three weeks since we'd begun our campaign.

We'd started by targeting Bonanno gambling dens. At first, we'd reported them to the police, but as is normal for Plan A, there were unforeseen complications. The police, rather than raiding the dens, had turned a blind eye and *notified* them instead. You hear about corrupt cops all the time, but you never really *believe* the stories, you know?

You wanna keep thinking the people being paid to protect you have your best interests at heart.

Plan B, though? A work of art. Absent the easy path to victory, I was forced to get *creative*. This time, we'd scoped out the games for several days and took note of the big winners.

Over the next few days, those winners had lost their newfound fortunes . . . but not at the gambling tables. The money they'd won vanished from their homes, their safes, their bank accounts. Some had found themselves cornered in alleyways and roughed up a bit to discourage them from investigating. But that hadn't stopped the rumors from spreading that the Bonannos themselves'd ordered it done. With Z fanning the flames and Addie planting a few choice pieces of evidence, the Bonanno family's gambling operations had quickly picked up a reputation of perilousness for anyone taking home too large a profit, and attendance had gone the way of the dinosaurs.

It was possible the mob might investigate. If

they suspected they had enemies, they'd try to track us down, and that wouldn't end happily for us. To keep the heat off, Z was spreading the rumor that the Bonanno gambling scene's collapse was the fault of a rogue element within the family itself, rather than an outside force. As far as we knew (meaning as far as Z'd told us), this'd been moderately successful, and several different in-groups were snapping at each other, passing the blame around like a jinxed necklace. The moment Z learned one group was becoming a pariah, we'd focus our efforts on them—try and pass our actions off as their rivals'.

Until then, that inner turmoil was the perfect scapegoat for the unlucky string of accidents the Bonanno *famiglia* had recently experienced.

My phone buzzed in my hand and I glanced down, trying to contort my face into a grimace of frustration. 1guy gettin up, not target tho

Followed quickly by, yea hes leaving

And, kira says ur plans r boring btw

Suddenly, that grimace of frustration was a whole lot less artificial.

The door opened and a thickset, swarthy man walked by me. I snuck as long a glance as I dared, committing his features to memory. He wasn't our target today, but remembering his face could always come in handy.

I opted against replying to Z—*someone* had to maintain a veneer of professionalism—but I'd think up something appropriately witty and caustic for next time Kira and I were face-to-face.

Today's target was the product of a full week's sleuthing on Addie's part. She'd been on several dozen recon missions over the last three weeks, and had identified the slender-shouldered, elderly man inside as an influential figure in the organization—not a capo, but treated with similar levels of respect. At his age, he could've retired from a once-held capo position years ago, but still helped out with the "family business." Removing him would deprive the Mafia of a wealth of valuable experience.

Addie'd tracked him to his house from a gambling den late one night, and had ducked out of school today to tail him again. He'd led her here, she'd called us, and we'd arrived with a plan concocted by yours truly.

We still didn't know his name (his fellow Mafiosos called him "The Barber"), but that was about to change.

I kept resolutely not looking at Addie *or* Kira's car until my phone buzzed again.

he paid. wallet in left pants pocket.

It was my job to get that information to Addie.

"It's not that hard," I said out loud, glaring at the screen and trying to imagine it'd eaten my unborn son. "A simple left turn, for Christ's sake!"

Left being the only important word I'd said.

Gotta send something to make it look like I'm communicating, I typed to Z.

The reply came almost immediately. <3

And then, seconds later, now.

"Son-of-a-bitch said he'd be here a fucking hour

ago!" I shouted in sudden frustration, spraying my phone with flecks of spit. A mom walking arm-in-arm with her kid turned completely around and gave me a look that indicated clearly her wish that I vanish from this earth.

Meltkraft's door opened again and two men—one young and stout, the other old and wispy-haired—stepped through it onto the sidewalk. Almost immediately, Addie flitted across my vision and collided full-force with the younger one. Given Addie's slim frame, this hardly moved her victim, but it *did* send her stumbling against the older man. The target.

"Oh God, I'm *so sorry!*" said Addie. It sounded like tears were welling in her eyes—she could make herself cry on command, as she often demonstrated when she was bored. We'd seen it dozens of times now, but she either didn't remember showing us or didn't care.

"Do not worry," said the man she'd collided

with gruffly, through a thick Italian accent. "No harm done, yes?"

I decided looking at them any longer could be suspicious and turned away. "Last time I show up on time for that asshole," I said for effect.

"Are you okay?" I heard Addie say. She sniffed loudly. "I'm such a clumsy—"

"No harm done," the other man repeated. His voice was higher, reedy. "Please forget it. Take a deep breath."

I heard several loud, exaggerated breaths. "Thank you!"

"It's no trouble at all," said the second voice. "Just relax a little. And have a lovely day."

"Thanks! You too!" called Addie as the two mobsters began to move again. They were just passing me when Addie yelled, "Wait, Mister! You dropped your wallet!"

The men turned around and I glanced up again to watch as Addie darted forward and shoved a small black leather wallet into the older man's hand.

"I'm sorry, I'm sorry, I'm sorry—"

"Oh, thank you!" he said genially. "Please, don't work yourself up." He gave her a gentle smile.

Addie turned bright red (which she can *also* do on command—she's one of the most talented actors I've ever met. Just one more reason why she's amazing), then did an about-face and fled.

"That poor woman," said the target as the two men passed me, walking slowly in the other direction. "Very stressed. Business does that to women."

I struggled to hide my traditional post-mission-accomplished smile since I was supposed to still be annoyed as hell at my fictional friend. I gave it three more minutes, then texted Z—all done—and shoved my phone into my pocket hard enough to rip the seam.

It'd almost been *too* easy—the hardest part'd been keeping my eyes off Addie, who somehow looked just as alluring despite looking like someone'd run her face through an aging program. But then, it'd been one of *my* plans. And my plans don't fail.

Forget those long, convoluted plots in heist movies. In real life, they'd fall apart in seconds because they require that so many things go exactly right. You can really only include three uncertainties in a plan before it becomes untenable. And since only an idiot trusts a plan that's only *barely* reliable enough, the real limit's *two*.

Pickpockets've bumped into their marks for centuries, and for good reason—it *works*. A little *too well*, in fact, as it's such an infamously effective technique, everyone knows about it. But over the years, it's boasted a pretty good success rate (exact statistics are unavailable, for reasons that should be obvious).

Another message from Z, confirming what I already knew. She got it

Whatever the statistics were, they'd just gone up by one.

TWO

I F ALL OF US, KIRA PROBABLY CARES MOST ABOUT keeping her family separate from the CPC. Addie uses her profits to keep her mom afloat financially, so even if her mom wouldn't approve, she couldn't say much if she found out. *I* couldn't give two shits what that asshole Lucas thinks, and Mom . . . isn't in a position to object, exactly. Z's dad's a cop (I suspect that's where Z gets his stupid morality), which could be trouble, but I don't think Z actually cares that much. Like, he recognizes it'd be bad if his parents found out, but it doesn't keep him up at night. Kira, though, *frets*—she'll do whatever it takes to keep her family's misconceptions carefully in place.

And yet, outside school, we almost always meet at Kira's house.

It makes sense, right? Kira drives us around, but it's not technically her car—her family needs it too. So she's not allowed to go somewhere else (say, my house) and just *stay* for hours. I've suggested she buy *herself* a car, but she always says her parents would ask where the money came from. To me, that just reflects her priorities—she'd rather risk them overhearing something at her house than make them suspicious by buying a car. But every time I explain this to Kira, it's like talking to a brick wall. A brick wall that's giving off the impression that it'll sock you in the face if you don't shut up. She still lets us in the door, though, so my arguments must get through on some subconscious level.

I think it's partly that to ensure privacy, Kira has no choice but to host us in her bedroom. And if *my* bedroom were as messy as hers, I know I wouldn't want my friends there. Currently, I was sharing a large wooden toy chest with a precarious pile of old binders, a broken lava lamp, and, for some reason, several bars of soap. *And* I had the cleanest spot—I knew I'd chosen well because Z kept sending envious glances my way.

"First things first," I began, surreptitiously wiggling away from a stray action figure. "Good job, team. Everything went off without a hitch . . . professionalism over the designated communication channels nonwithstanding."

"*Not*withstanding," said Addie. I shot her a dirty look, but she just winked at me.

"If our resident master thief would stop nitpicking about my pronunciation and hand over the ID . . . "

Addie reached into her pocket and tossed me the card. It spiraled through the air like a boomerang and struck me right in the chest. I clapped my hand over it before it fell.

"Vito DiGiovanni," I read. "On it, Kira?"

"Natch," said Kira. Her laptop was already open. "D-I, or D-E?"

"D-I."

"Righto."

I waggled the license at Addie. "Won't he miss this?"

Addie shrugged. "I didn't have time to deliberate over what to grab. You want my job so badly—"

It sounded waspish, but like my angry look earlier, there was no sting in it. We'd exchanged too many fleeting glances and secret touches over the past few weeks to take each other's petty irritation seriously.

Something felt . . . *right* about Addie. Looking at her, talking to her . . . hell, just *thinking* about her got me smiling. We hadn't exactly talked through our feelings yet, but we'd get our chance when the moment was right. Maybe when Addie finally made good on her promise to take me out to dinner, which—much like our talk—hadn't quite managed to materialize. Vengeance has a way of filling one's schedule. For example, I was supposed to be focusing on the next job, not wistfully contemplating my nebulous love life.

"You want *my* job?" I countered, trying to sound indignant. Addie was always at an advantage in these exchanges because she could *actually* sound angry or frustrated or offended, to the point where sometimes I worried I'd actually struck a nerve. And not only was I a worse actor, I was *also* worse at detecting insincerity, so she could always tell when I was posturing while I could rarely do the same. "I had to swear in a child's presence today. A mother *glared* at me. My conscience is stained forever."

Z stared at me thoughtfully. "Didn't *you* pick the phrase? Call me out if I'm wrong, but y'all remember that? I ain't making that up, right? He said it'd be funny."

"Just whose side are you on?"

"Hey, I ain't taking sides. Just reminding our master planner that *if* the plan called for loud cussing on a public sidewalk—"

"Incurring the wrath of passing mothers was easily avoidable," Addie agreed. "Jason, it's your *job* to notice pitfalls like this. I thought you said your plan was airtight. How could you not see this coming?"

Kira laughed. "That mom's gonna bust in here and spit your head on a kitchen knife, and you won't be alive to hear us blame you for ruining everything."

"Nobody's infallible," I muttered. And you must admit, that code phrase *had* been pretty funny.

"You know, maybe I *should* take your job," Addie mused. "So I can prevent fuckups of this magnitude in the future."

"Do you promise not to fuck me over?" asked Z. He had a point—I can't explain it, I don't ever intend it, but somehow, my plans *always* hand Z the short end of the stick. Yet he still hangs out with us. At this point, I'm not sure whether to admire his optimism or deride his inability to learn from the past.

But the guy's just a trouble magnet. Tell him to chat up some old friends in a bar and he'll get knocked out in a barfight. Make him the face of an illicit deal and the other guy'll be an undercover cop. Ask him if you can borrow a hundred dollars and while he's at the bank, a bank robber'll take him hostage.

Yes, all those things happened.

"I *would*," Addie demurred, "but there's no escaping your terrible karma."

"It ain't karma," said Z morosely. "God just hates me."

"I'm getting all sorts of shit," Kira interjected while we searched for a way to simultaneously sympathize with Z and laugh at him. "Home address, work address, Amazon reviews, the works. The guy loves his horses. And hey, check these wedding pics. Public album. Guess it's true what they say about old dudes and computers."

Z rolled his eyes. "Yeah, yeah. So anything actually important?"

"No, seriously. Look at the pics," said Kira. She turned the laptop around and we all moved closer, dodging stacks of paper and assorted dishware as we did.

Z wolf-whistled. "*Damn.*"

"She's so *young,*" said Addie.

"His third marriage, I think," said Kira. "Now c'mon, don't make me spell this out. You see it, right?"

Vito's wife *was* pretty, I had to admit—and my type. If you squinted, she almost looked like . . . oh.

I looked at Addie. Then back at the picture.

Addie noticed the path of my gaze. "Really? You think? No way, our mouths are *completely* different—"

"It *is* a stretch," I admitted. She'd need another wig, at the very least—it'd barely been a month since she'd cut her hair, and Vito's wife's went past her shoulders.

Now Z was catching on. "No, I see it. As long

as she doesn't have to fool any close friends. Or Vito himself. Wait, what's she gotta do, exactly?"

Addie sighed. "Someday, there'll be a job where I *don't* look like anyone involved. What will you do then?"

"I'm still figuring out that bit," said Kira to Z. "But there's a lot about this guy—I've barely scratched the surface. Gotta be some way to use it, but I dunno. Doesn't help that we're flying blind without a real plan."

"It *is* a real plan," I protested. "Just not an overarching one. How could I illustrate the details when we didn't know who this guy was, what he did, anything about him? Well, now we know, or *will*, and we can move forward."

"Yeah, but I dunno what stuff you'd give a shit about."

"Just send everything over e-mail and tell me anything that stands out right now. Actually, put it on this." I dug a flash drive out of my backpack. I'd grown up thinking e-mail was private, but it was time I permanently banished that idea. Flash drives are much more secure, and I promise I'm not being paid by the Flash Drive Lobby when I encourage you to use them habitually.

So. Again, we had options in the form of Vito's wife. I wasn't sure how to use that yet—kidnapping a prominent Mafioso's wife seemed clearly unfeasible—so I filed it safely away for potential later use.

"Got a report from Vincent," said Z quietly.

Vincent was one of Z's "contacts" within the mob. That's in quotes because he doesn't know he's feeding information to the enemy. To him, Z's just an old friend who's interested in criminal gossip. Z was pretty opposed to using him, but I wore him down eventually.

Sometimes, I can't decide if he's the CPC's moral center, or the most immoral of us all. Sure, he's constantly bringing up ethical concerns, but he always lets us shout him down and goes along with the plan anyway. Who's the worse person, the man who constantly goes against his principles, or the one who never had any to begin with?

"He says the capos are pissed," said Z, derailing my philosophical tangent. "Blaming each other, meeting behind each other's backs, making secret alliances, the works. The capo in charge of the card tables managed to come out looking pretty good, all things considered. Opportunistic son of a bitch, too—he leveraged the pushback against his rivals pretty smoothly, all but said flat out they'd set him up. Vince was pretty mad at one capo, Alberto Fettucci. That's who *he* thinks is behind it, and that's also the popular opinion. Alberto and Raffaele—that's the card capo—there's bad blood there, and Alberto's the kinda guy who'd do that sorta thing."

"Interesting." I thought through the scenario Z'd outlined, placing each party in their own mental box and thinking things over from their perspectives. "Has Alberto tried spinning it as a frame job by Raffale instead?"

It's what *I'd* do in his situation.

Z shrugged. "He didn't say."

"And the possibility that it's an outside group, do they suspect that?"

Another shrug. "If Vince didn't mention it, probably not."

"Next time you see him, can you name drop Vito DiGiovanni and see—?"

"I didn't wanna push him, dude. Like, it's bad enough he's telling me this stuff. If he thinks I'm actually digging for information, he'll clam up faster than you can say *omertà*."

Kira looked blankly at him. "And I'd say that because . . ."

"Oh, come *on*. The Mafia code of silence? That I explained like five times?" Z let out a long breath of exasperation. I knew that breath well—I stifle three or four every CPC meeting.

"I get it, Z," I said, and Z gave me a long-suffering look of relief. "Don't push him. The info's worth a ton as is. If you can't get more, we'll just have to—"

"Hold up," said Kira suddenly, jerking her head up from the computer, and then, "Oooh, whiplash."

I've learned to tolerate Kira's lack of manners. I tried improving them at first, but soon learned my folly. It's like teaching a bear to wear shoes—frustrating, sometimes painful, and ultimately useless.

"Um, what were those names? Rafael and Alberto Fettuccine?"

"*Raffale* and Alberto *Fettucci*," corrected Z.

"Right," said Kira, massaging her neck. "This New Yorker article mentions Alberto and Vito together. Check it out."

I wove my way through the hazardous room to Kira. "Belmont Stadium Relives Glory Days," I read out loud.

Kira jabbed a thumb at the screen. "There. 'But for New York residents Alberto Fettucci and Vito DiGiovanni, who have been coming to the track since nineteen seventy-eight, the crowds at Belmont are a happy return to the Golden Age of racing, when Secretariat blazed a trail of victories across the nation.' Told you the guy liked horses, boss."

I speed-read the rest of the article. Vito and Alberto popped up several times, always as living examples of the article's narrative. For the average reader, their names would've been unwelcome distractions at best. But to me, it painted a *very* clear picture of their relationship with the racetrack— and with each other.

"Did I do good? Like, can we use this?" asked Kira.

"Why, yes," I said, allowing myself the tiniest of smirks. "Yes, we can."

THREE

TWO DAYS LATER, WE WERE ROBBING A HOUSE. More specifically, Addie was robbing a house and the rest of us were on-site just in case. Kira held the prepaid cellphone we'd been talking to Vito with, and Z had a direct line to Addie in case something went wrong on either end. Not wanting to be left out, I too had a phone with a very specific purpose attached to it. And since I'd made the plan, I'd given myself the fun job.

"She's been in a while," Kira noted, looking at Z's phone. "You think maybe something happened?"

"It's fine," said Z. "She's still got six minutes."

Kira still looked worried, so he kept going. "Addie won't let herself get caught. She's too good."

"Besides, she can always just sneak past Vito," I pointed out. "Might not even need to sneak—he's pretty old. Probably can't hear too well."

We'd gotten Vito's number and address from the White Pages, and Addie'd called him after working herself into hysterics.

"Hello? Is this Vito DiGiovanni? Yeah, hi. I'm so sorry but I found your driver's license on the street! Yeah, I'm the girl you ran into. It fell out or something . . . "

By then, we'd already chosen our house. We needed something a decent but convenient distance away from Vito's—ten minutes was fine, we'd decided. From there, we'd searched for houses with multiple stories, few residents, and high socioeconomic indicators. Finally, we'd chosen a modest but well-made house in Jackson Heights that looked like it'd been assembled from five light-blue wooden blocks.

"I'm off work at six-thirty, so could you come by at six forty-five tomorrow? I'm so sorry, I'd come to you, but I don't have a car right now and I'm dealing with a really messy divorce, so I really can't afford to spend an hour taking the bus . . . "

Luckily—or perhaps due to Addie's theatrical talents—Vito was happy to oblige. It was still less hassle than the DMV, after all. (One of the plan's trouble spots had been the possibility that Vito would replace his license before Addie could contact him, but I'd been sure he'd avoid the DMV as long as possible, like all sane people.) Addie'd called him one last time before we left, just to double-check that Vito understood what he was supposed to do.

"And one more thing, I'll probably be listening to music with my headphones in. It's the only way I can get any cleaning done. Just walk in and make yourself at home. I'll be in the dining room or kitchen. I'll leave the door open."

Once Vito'd been dealt with, Addie could play

his wife a little more freely. I was still working out how to use that, but even if I couldn't, we'd still be putting a Mafioso in custody tonight, and that was a good few days' work.

I didn't wanna uncork the champagne just yet, but tonight could mark the beginning of a major victory. The more serious charges likely wouldn't stick, not with the lawyers someone with Vito's connections could conjure. But with any luck, those same connections would be revealed during the investigation, creating new leads for later investigation. With a little *more* luck, Vito would take a deal and throw his brothers under the bus. That last part was beyond my power to control, but I allowed myself the luxury of hope.

They should never've tried to kill Jason Jorgensen.

The opening front door jarred me out of my reverie. Moving like a deadly panther, Addie slipped through the crack (leaving it open for Vito) and descended the stairway step by painstaking step.

In her gloved hands, she held a small bag and a laptop case, and as she crossed the street towards us, I could make out her proud smile, the mark of a job well done.

"Jewelry," she said smugly, holding up the bag and shaking it a little. "Computer," she said, indicating the case. Without breaking stride, she walked past us into a gap between houses and crouched behind a garbage bin, becoming invisible to the rest of the street. That was our cue to scatter.

"Gentlemen, it's been lovely," said Kira as we spread out along the sidewalk.

Just a few minutes later, a silver Maserati rounded the corner and parked in front of the blue block-house. It looked like it existed in a permanent state of just-been-polished. Though I wasn't close enough to hear, I knew Kira'd just gasped enviously.

It was a beauty, but there was no time to admire its every bolt and rivet—my window was measured in seconds.

The number I dialed wasn't a long one, by any means. Three simple digits.

"Hello?" I said in hushed tones. "I think my neighbor's being robbed!" I hyperventilated a bit for effect. "There's a strange man at her door. He was fumbling around for the key, and I've never seen him before. He's wearing," I glanced over at Vito, who'd just gotten out of his car on the passenger side, "gray slacks and a button-up white shirt."

"Don't panic. Are you certain he isn't supposed to be there?" The operator sounded sympathetic, but utterly, eerily calm. I wondered idly how often she'd practiced that voice.

"I'm sure!" I hissed. "He's old, I don't think she knows anyone that old. Besides, she's never home this time of night. The house is empty!"

That wasn't necessarily true, but I didn't care as long as it got the police here. It'd been empty at this time *yesterday*, but one data point wasn't indicative, and we'd lacked the time for a proper stakeout.

I heard a small beep, and then "What's your location?"

"My neighbor lives at forty-two Ninety-Third Street," I said. "Queens."

Another beep. "I've dispatched an officer to your location."

"Okay, thanks so much, bye!" I said fast and breathlessly, then hung up before the operator could ask anything or request I stay on the line.

I turned my attention back to the house. Vito'd reached the porch. He saw the open door, opened it all the way, and stepped inside. The moment he was gone, Addie straightened up from behind the bin and walked briskly toward the car, stolen items in hand. I moved to intercept her.

"Vito's got a driver," I muttered, drawing abreast of her.

Addie stopped dead, and her eyes flicked towards the driver's tinted window. "You sure?"

"He got out on the passenger side."

"And we're on a time limit." Addie looked up at the house, then back at the car. Caught between them. "No evidence, no case! You know that!"

"What do we . . . " I looked at her helplessly, waiting for her to supply an idea, but she just looked back at me, lips pressed together tightly.

Right. *I* was the idea-guy. That was *my* responsibility.

"Follow my lead."

I wheeled around, back towards the car, and walked up to the window. I rapped on it, still unsure of what I'd say. In my peripheral vision, I saw Addie move quietly around behind the car. Good to see she'd picked up on the plan.

Slowly, the window rolled down.

"Hey, you in there!" I said loudly—not shouting, I didn't want Vito hearing—as soon as I had a crack to speak through. "What are you doing parking in my spot, huh?"

I ran the words together, trying to create a

wall of noise without any gaps of silence. Addie crouched by the passenger door opposite me and vanished from my sightline.

The man inside glared with sharp, diamond eyes. "Excuse me . . . *your* spot?"

"Damn right it's my spot!" I fired back. "Everyone on the block knows it's my spot. Even the *garbage man* knows it's my spot! I park my car every day right between these two trees, and I don't care how fancy or expensive your car is, Mister, its back half is hanging over my space!"

I took the fastest breath I could and plunged on, like a pompous congressman mid-filibuster, not letting his political opponents get an opposing word in. "What's the idea, anyway? Do you rich types get off coming into my neighborhood and parking anywhere you damn well please?"

"Listen, you," growled the driver, but I didn't let him speak. The ever-louder police sirens in the distance were a constant reminder of our dwindling time.

"Were you born with a silver spoon in your mouth? Got the entire street in front of *your* house cordoned off? Well, I won't stand for it! I may just write the *Times*. In fact, I think I *will* write the *Times*! What's your license plate number?"

I paused at last for breath and the wailing sirens filled the vacuum of silence. There's *no way* he didn't hear them. Behind the car, Addie rose back into view and flashed me a thumbs up.

Vito's driver was practically apoplectic. "You want my plates for a letter to the *Times*? How old *are* you? You even old enough to drive?"

Addie, minus jewelry and laptop, started walking down the sidewalk like she was on a twilight stroll. I decided to follow her lead and extricate myself.

"Whoops, sorry," I said, "You aren't in my spot at all. I'm thinking of *those* two trees, not these two." I gestured apologetically at a pair of trees about ten yards down. "Bye!"

I hurried back across the street, a lone figure

against the setting sun. Kira and Z were long gone, and it was well past time to join them.

Two police cars rounded the corner and drove right past me. I watched from a safe distance as they parked in the street, lights flashing a warning. Four officers hopped out of the cars. One was speaking rapidly into a radio.

Vito's driver got out too, and started towards the clump of officers. One split off to intercept his approach while the rest walked up the steps.

I gotta give old Vito credit—he knew better than to try and run, or resist arrest. He hadn't survived in the Mafia this long by being stupid, that's for sure. Before the policemen could open the door, he stepped out with his hands above his head. I couldn't decipher his expression at this distance, so I'm not sure how composed he was as an officer tightened handcuffs around his wrists. He was certainly less agitated than his driver, who was red-faced and shaking an angry fist at the officer who'd been assigned to block him.

I made myself scarce before the police started looking for the "neighbor" who'd called in the robbery. The sounds of the confrontation faded behind me into the cool night air.

Kira and Z were waiting two blocks down, where we'd left her car.

"Addie's circling around the block to avoid the kerfuffle," said Kira. "Thought you should know, so you don't kill yourself worrying over your sweetie-pie."

I rolled my eyes. "Let's pick her up and make ourselves scarce."

I knew she'd pout at my not taking the bait, but if I'd known she wouldn't *stop* pouting the whole way home, maybe I would've indulged her.

FOUR

"**Y**OU'RE KIDDING ME."

"Nope."

"She *didn't.*"

"She absolutely did."

I rested my forehead against the cool wood of the table. "I need a drink."

"There I can't help you," said Z solemnly. "Not being dumb enough to bring booze into school. But I know a guy who knows—"

"It's an *expression.*"

I'd sent Kira and Z to snoop around Belmont Park for more information on Vito and Alberto. In all fairness, they'd exceeded my expectations in *that* regard—Z's friend at the racetrack had been a gold mine of gossip. Problem is, they'd exceeded my expectations other ways too. Namely, in how many horses they'd purchased in the process.

I say *they*, but Z'd played no part in this madness. It was Kira alone who deserved the blame, and Kira alone who now apparently owned a horse. Must've found a two-for-one deal on smug looks too, given the number she'd been sending my way from a couple seats down. I was trying to ignore them by staring at Professor Gildfin, the CPC's official mascot/club faculty sponsor, as he drifted idly around his bowl, but she wasn't fooled.

I wasn't sending Z and Kira on a mission together without supervision *ever* again. I could practically *see* how it'd played out—Z trying to be the voice of reason but ultimately losing through a combination of wanting to avoid bodily harm and being unable to resist Kira's magnetism. But what I *couldn't* imagine was . . .

I locked eyes with Kira. "*Horses?*"

She shrugged. "I've always wanted to rain blows down upon my enemies from a horse's back. With a lance, or a sword, or something."

"That . . . makes a lot of sense, actually."

"That's what *I* said," said Z.

"What's his name?" asked Addie, running her fingers through the dark-haired wig I'd tossed her when the meeting started.

"Summer Disaster," said Kira proudly. "He placed at the race we watched. *And* cost Z ten bucks, which is even better."

I took a deep breath, tried to wrench my mind back to the relevant intel Z'd gotten from his bookie buddy and shared with us. But the thought *Kira has a pet horse* kept pushing itself back into the forefront of my mind, demanding to be dealt with—even though dealing with it wasn't my job.

It's intensely frustrating to know you're being irrational, yet still being unable to stop yourself.

"What'll you tell your parents?" I asked.

Kira grimaced. "I dunno yet, but I'm thinking

it over. Maybe I just *won't*. Not like they have to know—I've got the cash to keep him myself."

If I had children someday, I'd now be forever wondering if they had a secret horse I didn't know about.

"It's like an investment," said Kira with a grin. "I get part of the purse whenever he at least shows. I worked it all out with Jack—Jack's his jockey. I'm letting him stay on and race . . . "

Kira's words faded to empty noise in my ears as I forced everything horse-related out of my head, once and for all.

I hadn't needed to look farther than the third page of the *Times* to discover Vito's fate, but I'd needed more detailed information, so I'd called his lawyer pretending to be a journalist. After promising I'd take a sympathetic stance in my upcoming article, he'd given me the particulars I needed.

The stolen objects'd been found in his car, and his driver's belligerence hadn't helped matters. Despite this, the goods were clean of his fingerprints, and while their owner was eager to pursue trespassing charges, Vito was insistent that a transcript of his recent phone logs would clear his name—which, of course, they would. We'd destroyed the phone Addie'd used, of course—the same night as Vito's arrest—but the logs would be safe, tucked away in some NSA databank.

I didn't know how they'd affect the verdict if released, though. Vito could prove he'd been framed, but would have trouble providing a motive without violating *omertà*. The Mafia didn't like involving the law in their disputes, and for good reason. If Vito wanted to punish the guilty party, he'd have to pursue a personal vendetta . . . once he was released. With any luck, that'd be a while.

And if *that* weren't enough to think on, there was Z's information, mercifully delivered *before* the equine bombshell'd been dropped. Turns out that after *The New Yorker* article, Vito and Alberto were Belmont racetrack celebrities—practically permanent fixtures at the races, popular with the other regulars and always ready with a bet. But while Alberto liked betting high, he relied on Vito to place those bets. Without Vito, Z's friend'd told him, Alberto'd be floundering.

The two were obviously good friends, so Alberto probably knew Vito's wife—I gave it ninety to ninety-five percent odds. But *she* apparently wasn't known around Belmont, so how well could he know her, really? Probably just a passing familiarity. Gun to my head, I'd bet Addie could pull it off. That was . . . probably relevant, somehow.

I tried thinking back through what I knew about Alberto himself. Z'd said he was the new scapegoat among the capos. Might that stress lead to longer hours at Belmont? Larger, riskier bets, perhaps? It seemed likely—or at least plausible.

But from this soup of possibilities, no obvious path suggested itself. The data was a web of branching lines mixed with unknown variables, combining into semi-coherent structures with odds of success that fluctuated second-to-second depending on how I squinted at them. All too ephemeral to be useful.

"Do I need more information?" I wondered out loud.

It was a mistake. For in speaking, I reflexively focused my hearing, anticipating a response. And that opened my ears to "Kira's Horse Talk Show," Live from Room 206, Van Buren High.

" . . . And the owner was *so* nice. He's actually been trying to sell Summer Disaster for *months*, can you believe that? He wasn't doing well lately, so it was a big surprise when he got second today. But now I'm gonna drive down every weekend and bet on him and—"

And just like that, the plan coalesced—popped out of my head fully formed, like Athena from Zeus's brow. "Thanks, Kira," I said over her monologue. "I've got it."

Kira looked like she couldn't decide whether to ask me to clarify, or punch me in the eye for cutting her off. She took some deep breaths, and the former inclination overpowered the latter.

It was the most *un-Kira* thing she'd ever done. Kira doesn't back down from a slight, and she *certainly* doesn't try to calm herself by breathing. That's like Z deciding he has enough friends. I was reminded of Kira's weirdness in Vegas, and how I'd never solved the mystery of *why*.

It looked like she'd just actually *tried to calm herself down*.

Come to think of it, I hadn't seen her so much as *shove* someone since we'd returned from Las Vegas. She talked as big a game as ever, but the follow-through was . . . missing. Like she'd become all bluster overnight.

I've seen Kira in action. She's anything *but* bluster.

In my business, bodily injury's an omnipresent threat. You take it seriously, in other words—you don't wanna be blindsided when the gloves come off, or you're practically dead. My plan's always to let Kira loose on whoever's threatening us . . . and she'd always been happy to oblige. But if she *wasn't*, that could easily explain the Kosmos Lounge fiasco.

What about the hit men? Could she have turned the tables on them? Had she held back?

No, of course not. This was *Kira*, after all. Whatever was up with her, she'd never value non-violence over her own *life*.

But she wouldn't have had to make that choice— just convince herself I had a plan and remove the burden of responsibility from her own shoulders. Kira has her faults, but lacking faith in me isn't one of them. She could've convinced herself, no problem.

Was Kira the adrenaline junkie becoming a secret *pacifist?*

I'd have a heart-to-heart with her as soon as was convenient. Or maybe ask Addie to do it for me— Kira and I've been friends since freshman year, but she and Addie'd bonded incredibly fast. Factor in

Addie's social sense, and she was probably a better choice.

But for now, I pretended I hadn't noticed anything unusual. "You'll like it." I grinned. "We're gonna buy another horse."

There was shocked silence from the entire table, broken finally by Kira's bark of laughter. "I knew you were alright, boss," she chuckled. "Always looking out for me."

"It's gotta be a fast one," I continued, secretly reveling in Z's and Addie's confusion. "That means expensive. It could represent our entire war chest, or more."

Six hundred thousand dollars from the Vegas caper'd gone into a communal fund for use against the Mafia. It was mostly intact, just begging to be put to use.

"I'll cover the difference out of pocket," I assured them. "But I wanna get your approval before I go spending."

Z frowned. "Can I hear the plan first? But if

you need a good horse, I can set you up with someone—"

"*Seriously?*" muttered Addie.

"—Dale, don't worry, he's chill. He breeds horses for fun and cash. Fair prices, but he owes me, so I could score a deal. You know, if I had to."

He tilted his chair back and put his feet up on the table.

"I just wanna make sure we're all on the same page," I said. "We've fucked around with the Mafia's profit streams, minor members, et cetera. Fine, whatever. But this time, we're targeting a capo. That's a significant escalation. If Alberto falls, they'll be spooked. They catch wind of our involvement—or even suspect it—and they won't pull any punches. Understand?"

I spoke mainly for Kira's benefit, but I avoided looking at her. Hopefully, the message was clear— *I'm relying on you to throw down if necessary, so you'd better be ready when the time comes.*

But Kira just laughed again. "You fucking know it. When do I get to kick ass?"

Had she reacted too slowly or too quickly? Was the emotion behind the words at any point less than genuine? Or was I jumping at shadows, imagining problems that didn't really exist?

Addie weighed in next. "The way I see it, as long as we stay under the radar, we're fine. The moment we get found out, we're dead. That's our situation *now*, and going after a capo doesn't change that. We made this decision weeks ago already, so unless anyone's thinking about quitting while we're ahead—"

"Nah," said Z. "That ain't an option."

His eyes darkened, and I knew he was thinking back to that night in Vegas. Alone in the all-consuming blackness. No sound but our breathing and the wind across the dunes. The terror of knowing that if the man behind you wanted you dead, you *would* be before the gunshot's *crack* made it to your ears. Walking farther and farther from any hope of rescue into the shifting desert that would be your grave, because you had no choice.

Someone'd set us up to be in that position from the beginning. And it was our *responsibility* to give that someone what they deserved, no matter the risk. In that moment, I could see in Z's face that he felt the same way.

I waited a little longer, but nobody else said anything.

"Guess we're all agreed."

"All *right*," said Kira. "Now, tell us about the other horse!" She was practically giddy with anticipation.

"Please," said Addie. She kept her face perfectly serious, but I heard the wry humor behind her words (though probably only because she was letting me). "Tell us how doubling Kira's new herd is going to break the New York Mafia in half."

"Ladies and gentleman—and fish—prepare yourselves. This plan's gonna blow your motherfucking minds."

I could tell they weren't impressed—which is fair, since I say stuff like that all the time. But I'm still full of surprises, and it was time to remind them of that.

"Z, you know any arms dealers?"

Z looked taken aback, but only for a second. Then he smiled widely.

FIVE

OUT OF EVERYWHERE I'VE BEEN, A HORSE'S STALL ranks in *at least* the bottom ten.

It's not just the smell and the crap, though that's easily enough to make it bottom fifty material. No, what really clinches it is the horse—in this case, a brown stallion named Sanderson. Stalls aren't built to contain a horse *and* two teenagers, so space is an issue. Because of this, the horse isn't in a very good mood and you get the sense that he'll lash out with his hind legs any second.

Kira'd made sure we understood *exactly* how damaging a horse's kick could be, and the image she'd conjured was still fresh in my mind. There was a lot of squirming around trying to avoid touching Sanderson—while also avoiding his leavings—as he moved about the enclosure, just in case getting under his hooves made him start kicking. *Plus*, horses are giant natural furnaces, so it was also uncomfortably warm. Z was gingerly avoiding brushing against the horse, the walls, *or* the feeding trough, so concerned was he about the cleanliness of his green silk jacket. Technically, it was just a costume piece, but he'd taken to it immediately . . . and he hadn't stopped giving me his "I'm suffering and you're to blame" look since we'd opened the stall.

We couldn't even talk to pass the time, just in case someone was nearby. Our newly-bought horse's certificate of ownership'd gotten us this far, but technically, we weren't supposed to be here. In fact, if someone *did* open the stall, I'd have to make a new plan very quickly. We'd done our best to confirm that Sanderson's handlers were occupied elsewhere, but we didn't know where they'd gone or when they might return. You're probably thinking *what a shitty plan*, and honestly, I can't disagree. It's the kind of plan that Lucas would probably *disown* me for. It being crazy enough to work didn't lessen the sheer number of ways it could fail.

Still, the wait wasn't without its entertainment. Our Bluetooth headsets were connected to a mic hidden on Addie's person. It wasn't too powerful, so unless someone else was *really* close to her or yelling, her voice was all we could hear. For the last hour, we'd been listening to half a conversation as Addie, dolled up to look like Vito DiGiovanni's youthful wife, prattled on about all manner of inane crap.

The longer she talked, the more danger she was in. It'd only take one mistake to blow her cover. But she seemed comfortable enough, and if I'd been able to hear the whole conversation, I'd have no doubt appreciated the artistry with which Addie steered away from uncomfortable areas, picked up conversational cues, and wormed her way out of suspicion whenever she slipped up.

It also would've helped to understand Italian.

Kira'd left us at Belmont in the early morning, then drove off to monitor Vito's wife and make sure she didn't interact with Alberto—which I didn't find likely, but extra caution never hurt. If Alberto got a call from Vito's wife while sitting right next to her, he'd know immediately that something was up.

Once Vito's *real* wife was under surveillance, Addie'd dialed Alberto. They'd commiserated over Vito's legal trouble, but Addie'd assured him that legally, things were in his favor, though the circumstances surrounding the trespassing charge were a little odd. And the timing was *terrible*, since Vito'd *just* bought him a present, but'd been arrested before he could give it.

That got Alberto's attention at once, and soon Addie'd arranged to meet him at Belmont Racetrack to present the gift in her "husband's" stead. She concluded the call by saying that while bail was slow in coming, she was confident it'd be granted and that Vito'd be joining Alberto on the racetrack again before long (this was unfortunately true—Kira was stalling the process wherever possible, but all the computer tricks in the world couldn't hold it back forever).

The promise of a gift was also genuine, and it was the most expensive gift I'd ever purchased. Even with Z's connections, my pockets were almost one and a half million dollars lighter. The war chest was empty, my own assets were drained, and I'd been forced to sell some stock to finance the rest of the operation—including the headsets (which I was confident were well worth the investment) and Z's one hundred percent authentic jockey uniform (which he'd fallen in love with).

When I'd seen the price tag, I'd wanted to back out, find a different way, fool Alberto into *thinking* we'd given him a horse, with fake paperwork or something. But there was no way around it—Alberto needed to *really* have that horse. For it was Addie who was giving it to him, and it was Addie he needed to trust for the plan to work. If he tried visiting "his" horse and got turned away, that was it. And so—reluctantly—I'd signed the check. In exchange for more money than the average family made in two decades, I was now the proud owner of Roger-De-Coverly, a noble racehorse with an impressive pedigree, and would remain his owner for *at least* five more minutes.

When Addie finally suggested that they visit the stables, we snapped to attention. Z stood slowly, lifting his head above the wooden half-door. Sanderson snorted softly at the human head slowly rising beside him. "Clear," said Z.

"Let's hope it stays that way," I said.

"Have you decided which horse you'll bet on?" I heard in my ear. As always, I didn't hear Alberto's response, just silence while Addie listened.

"Yes, he's very good. Well, don't worry. I'll help you instead. Roger-De-Coverly's the smart pick."

Being unable to hear half the conversation was frustrating, but I could figure out the other half decently well if I thought about it. Part of me wondered if Addie was intentionally phrasing her replies so I could fill in the blanks, but she couldn't possibly be keeping *that* in her head on top of everything else . . . right?

" . . . First-class pedigree, Vito says. Got the X-factor from War Admiral—the large heart, you know. All the indicators of health and speed—nice sheen, high crest. And, of course, he's yours."

I allowed myself to imagine Alberto's look of surprise and amazement—had to get *something* for my money, after all.

"Yes, yours. I've got the deed right here. For the friendship you've shown Vito over the years. No, of course. You're quite welcome. Good. Please do."

I stood too and moved next to Z as Addie basked in the glow of Alberto's gratefulness. He wanted to know everything about his horse—its mother and father, its measurements in hands, its previous owner . . . the questions flowed unceasingly. Addie fielded them one by one, never losing patience.

"No, not yet, but we expect he will within his first three races. Ah yes, just a little further back."

That was our signal. I adopted an angry glower and looked down my nose at a suddenly uncertain Z.

"And I'm telling *you* it's too late," I snarled. "We've got all the favorites in our pocket—you gonna write 'em off? There's no refund."

Because I'd been specifically listening for it, I heard the door open halfway through my sentence. I pretended I hadn't.

"It's dangerous," said Z. "I don't wanna get put away. You know what they do to guys like us?"

"No one's getting put away. Not if you man up and keep your fat mouth shut. Can you handle that? These jocks are gonna feed you the win like Momma's porridge, so don't sweat it."

I swear I could hear Alberto's breathing from where I was standing, and I couldn't even hear

Addie's through the headset. It took all my will-power not to glance his way.

"And if someone blabs?"

"Trust me, kiddo. I've been doing this for years. They know what happens if they blab." Not that *I* did, but a little ominous ambiguity never hurt, right?

Z took a few deep, calming breaths. "Alright. I trust you, I do. I do. Gimme the shocker."

I reached into my pocket. Addie and Alberto couldn't see that low due to the stall door—which was handy, since I didn't actually have a shock device.

"Remember, only use it if a horse we didn't buy pulls ahead. And hold it like *this*, or the crowd'll see. And if they do . . . " I let the sentence hang as a threat. "Get me?"

"I get you," stammered Z, pretending to take something out of my hand.

"Hey, you'll do fine, kiddo. Just remember the payoff. Ride Sanderson over the line first and we go home rich."

"And you ain't never been caught before?"

I was about to respond when I heard Addie's voice in my ear . . . and not in the room.

"Under the circumstances," she was saying in a soft, conspiratorial voice, "I won't be offended if you don't bet on Roger."

Z heard it too, of course, and immediately straightened up out of his slouch, wiping beads of sweat off his forehead—real sweat.

"Finally," he said. "I was running outta things to say. Let's finish up before someone else comes in."

"No, don't tell them," said Addie. "Can't you see the opportunity?"

I pulled two small sponges and a box of sugar cubes out of my backpack. "Good boy," I said, patting Sanderson on the nose.

"How do you think Vito built *his* fortune?"

I reached into my ear and pulled out the headset with a quick twisting motion. This task required concentration.

"Z, watch the hallway," I said, handing him the

headset. He opened the stall and stationed himself by the door. Sanderson poked his head towards freedom, but I stood squarely in his path. "Easy there."

I fed him a sugar cube—it was only polite, considering what I was about to put him through. Then I slowly began easing a sponge into his left nostril, feeding him another cube with my other hand. He shied away, ignoring the sugar—much like you'd ignore a Jolly Rancher if someone were shoving a sponge up *your* nose.

"Easy," I muttered again, wishing Kira were here to wrestle the horse to the ground or something. I tried again, this time holding the sponge against his nostril for a bit to get him used to the sensation. Then, as Sanderson breathed in deeply, I shoved it in with my thumb.

Sanderson whinnied and reared. Two hooves rose past my head and my life flashed before my eyes.

I threw myself backwards through the stall door, which Z'd thankfully (though irresponsibly) left open. As Sanderson came down again, I threw myself against the door and latched it before the distressed stallion could burst out into the stable. The second sponge, which had been resting on the door, rolled off—on my side of the divide, thankfully. I grabbed it.

"Let's go!" I said as Sanderson whinnied again in discomfort. I couldn't help but feel sorry for the poor horse, but if there'd been a more optimal way to play this, I hadn't seen it.

I ran past Z into the hallway he'd been watching and he followed, matching my pace. Neither of us were eager to be here if and when the commotion drew jockeys—or worse, security. We slowed to a brisk walk once we'd reached the end of the hallway. There were several people walking one way or another, but none were moving urgently toward Sanderson's stall, so I figured we were clear. One waved at Z—"Hey, Zephyr! Didn't know you raced!"—but he thankfully seemed too busy to start a conversation.

"You get them in?" said Z once we'd put a few minutes of distance between us and the stall.

"One," I said. "Son-of-a-bitch almost trampled me. If you want, you can go back and do the other."

"I'm good," said Z. "It better be enough, though, because Addie's pretty much convinced him. Took her awhile, but it's all good now."

He handed my headset back and I repositioned it carefully in my ear while Z shielded me from view.

" . . . All of it?" Addie was saying. "You *are* guaranteed to win."

I crossed my fingers behind my back.

"And you could buy my husband *his* own horse too."

Z and I looked at each other expectantly.

"Took you long enough," said Addie, and then something in Italian I couldn't understand.

We broke out into identical grins.

SIX

WE HAD TIME TO KILL BEFORE OUR RACE BEGAN, so we explored the track a little, got lunch at a sandwich vendor's, then checked out the paddock where the horses were being paraded before the race. Sanderson was among them, looking none the worse for wear, though his nostrils were flared slightly.

I'd read that a sponge in each nostril could reduce a horse's oxygen intake by up to fifty percent. I wasn't sure how the absence of one sponge affected that number, but I hoped the answer was "not *significantly*." I also hoped Kira never found out I'd done that—she didn't know, and I certainly wasn't gonna tell her.

By the paddock's edge, Roger-De-Coverly pranced for his audience. His eyes were bright and energetic, and I found myself drawn to bet on him. I didn't, of course, as betting's *always* rigged against you (if it weren't, the venue couldn't pay its property taxes). Plus, I was incredibly low on cash—though not as low as Alberto was about to be.

Addie'd excused herself to the bathroom and used the time alone to give me the Cliff's Notes of the part of the conversation I'd missed. Alberto'd been reluctant to use his "inside knowledge" and had wanted to notify the racetrack officials. Addie'd pointed out that Vito rigged races all the time, somehow managed to backpedal when Alberto'd known she was lying, then carefully and concisely laid out the case for using the information he'd "stumbled upon." And even after she'd convinced him to bet, she'd kept talking until he was ready to bet *big*—eight million, seven-hundred-forty thousand dollars big, or the entirety of his liquid assets *plus* a little extra.

No *way* could Alberto recover from a financial blow that big. Not without some amount of time— time he wouldn't have once word spread that the most unpopular capo was functionally bankrupt.

"Why're we here again?" Z muttered. Every inch of him, from his glassy-eyed stare to the slump in his shoulders to his leaden feet, screamed boredom.

"To see if anyone notices something's up with Sanderson," I muttered back.

We waited a little longer, but the crowd's dull murmur made eavesdropping practically impossible. We also weren't allowed in the paddock, so we both decided—separately but concurrently—that as nobody'd jumped up and shouted, "That horse can't breathe!" we were probably fine.

It wouldn't do if Alberto noticed that the horse he'd be betting the house on was uncharacteristically listless, so Addie distracted him from going to the paddock with a very long, dull story about her struggle against a tenacious, endlessly regenerating to-do list. By the time she let it end, he had barely enough time to make his ill-advised bet . . . and I was almost catatonic with boredom.

We chose our seats strategically, just four rows back and to the left of Addie and Alberto, who were sitting together in the second row. We had an almost perfect vantage point of the starting line. The horses were mostly lined up at the gate, only waiting on a few stragglers.

Z's face was obscured behind a copy of the *Telegraph*, but I couldn't tell if he was actually reading it or just trying to blend in. I nudged him.

"Dude, nobody's reading that shit now. You'll miss the race."

Z sighed loudly, but he lowered the paper. "Whatever. I didn't get it anyway."

The crowd's energy swelled and their excited murmurs peaked as the last horse took his place at the gate. Just as the buildup was becoming unbearable, the bell rang and the stands erupted in cheers.

"Aaaand they're off!" said the announcer. His voice was incredible, somehow simultaneously full of excitement and bereft of all feeling. "Strong start by Trump Card, with Count Claria passing on the inside. Love Commander fourth, making a strong bid for third. Roger-De-Coverly . . . "

I craned my neck, seeking the deep brown coat of the stallion that'd briefly been mine. There he was, an almond flash hugging the inside wall. He tried to cut between two neck-and-neck horses, but one veered right, blocking him. He dropped back temporarily, seeking another opening.

"Love Commander in second now, and they're at the curve."

The crowd was cheering themselves half to death, waving programs, ticket stubs, and bare fists at the track. I got the impression I should be joining in, but when I tried, I felt stupid and out of place, so I stopped.

Sanderson was doing pretty well, all things considered. He was holding steady near the back, but he wasn't ceding his position either. Alberto watched him motionlessly, not sparing even a glance for the other racers. Sanderson dominated his attention to the exclusion of all else as he awaited the comeback.

As the distance between the stands and the horses grew, the race became harder to follow, and listening to the announcer ("Caller," as the program named him) became a lot more compelling. Not that the relative lack of visibility discouraged the fans from their full-throated cheering.

"Standstill three lengths from the leader, Love Commander, and aiming for the outside to pass. Sanderson making up lost ground, coming up behind Morgan's Mane, and . . . he's now in sixth place, fighting Morgan's Mane for fifth."

Addie cheered—not too enthusiastically, not like a dedicated fan, but like someone who'd been to the racetrack enough to understand its social norms. She gave Alberto a nudge, trying to get him engaged in the cheering, but he sat perfectly still, staring at the racetrack like . . . well, like he had millions riding on the outcome. I wasn't sure if her eagerness was entirely an act, or if there was some truth to it, but either way I wished it was her, not grumpy-faced, unenthusiastic Z, next to me. Maybe when we had time, we could return, just us, and have a proper day at the races.

Maybe that'd get me cheering.

The horses reached the far turn, with Count Claria now in first. Sanderson was practically out of the race by now, flagging, winded. His jockey'd pushed him too hard, and he'd ceded most of the distance he'd gained in his fight to sixth. I couldn't see Alberto's face, but had no problem imagining his expression.

"They've entered the final three furlongs, with Count Claria leading by a hair against the rail, Love Commander in second and Standstill making a break on the outside. Roger-De-Coverly fourth and gaining!"

The announcer's voice was rising to a close facsimile of excitement as the horses neared the wire. His commentary came fast and frantic as the crowd readied their tickets to throw. They shouted over each other as they urged their favorites on, blending the names together into an indecipherable roar.

"Love Commander lagging, Standstill passes him on track for first. This could be the comeback!"

Count Claria's jockey was bent double over his horse's neck, urging him on for those final few seconds as the horses galloped towards us.

"He's across the wire! Count Claria takes it. Standstill was in second. Love Commander in third. Again, Count Claria in first, Standstill in second, and Love Commander in third."

With a final shout, worthless ticket stubs littered the stands like falling snow. Fans descended on the jockeys, shouting questions, showering praise, hurling abuse. But Alberto Fettucci stayed seated, perfectly still.

There was buzzing in my ear—crowd-babble filtered through a microphone. But as the din quieted, Addie's voice separated from the interference.

" . . . Help. I'll get the details from Vito, but the meeting's tomorrow night, at one a.m."

"She's planted the bait," I said.

Z looked at me contemptuously. "I *know*. I'm hearing everything you are."

Right.

"I will make this right. It is my promise to you."

Here's a tip, absolutely free. If someone loses you almost nine million dollars and then offers you a priceless business opportunity, refuse. Odds are they don't have your best interests at heart. That, or they're frighteningly incompetent, which should have similar implications for their trustworthiness.

"Good job today," I said, and Z fist-bumped me. I stood up, stretched my shoulders. It felt like *I'd* just run a race, rather than just watched it.

On the field, handlers were examining Sanderson. The sponge would be discovered eventually, and no doubt its discovery would make the failed multi-million dollar bet even more suspicious and noteworthy. But by the time word spread, it'd be too late.

Or so we hoped.

Racetrack policy was to not refund bets in the event of foul play. For Alberto, a track veteran, they might be moved to make a public exception—especially given the bet's size.

But a decision like that wouldn't be made in the next forty-eight hours.

That was plenty of time to contact him, set up a meeting, then—of course—stab him in the back.

Figuratively.

SEVEN

YOU'D THINK I'D BE USED TO BEING UNDERES-
timated due to my age by now, but it
somehow still catches me unaware. Sometimes,
they try to hide it, but Alberto Fettucci made no
such attempt—the amusement in his anemic smile
as he looked me over was clear as a summer day.

That was one reason I'd chosen such a dark
venue—to obscure my youth, at least a little. And
my appearance. And that we numbered only four,
all my age.

I had many things I'd prefer hidden, is my point.

The other reason, of course, was that for clandes-
tine deals, shadowy warehouses are *traditional.*

Here was the part that'd required a real horse. Addie'd needed to stay trustworthy all the way up to this meeting, or Alberto would simply cancel. Not only that, he'd know someone'd tried to snow him—he'd likely figure *that* out the second he thanked Vito for the gift, but why not prolong that day as long as possible?

Unfortunately, handing the guy we needed to be penniless a one-and-a-half-million-dollar asset had been unavoidable. But as long as "Mrs. DiGiovanni" was around to be offended at Alberto's putting Roger-De-Coverly up for sale when she was offering him a *perfectly* suitable job, selling him would be off the table. And after tonight, once it no longer mattered, Roger-De-Coverly was scheduled to make a daring escape from his paddock and make the journey to freedom, courtesy of Addie.

But that was all in the future. I had to make it through the meeting first.

"I was expecting someone with a little hair on

his chin," Alberto said at last. "Don't you have homework to do?"

It was a solid attempt at controlling the conversation from the beginning, especially because he was technically correct—AP classes aren't very forgiving, and I had test-prep worksheets waiting at home. But I was willing to accommodate his posturing. I'm happy playing the lower-status part in negotiations, because that's all it is—a play, an act. None of it actually matters except for who wins. And because I know that, I usually *do*.

"Mr. Eisl—ah, my employer, couldn't make it," I replied, keeping my face in shadow. I spoke quickly, like I was embarrassed I'd almost given away an important name. The more inexperienced Alberto thought I was, the better. "He thought I could use the experience, so he sent me instead."

I peered into the darkness of the warehouse like I could see someone there—an accomplice, say, whose hiding place I would've just revealed had he existed. In reality, that spot contained only a stack of boxes and a miniature forklift. Z was by the crates we'd brought, watching for foul play. Kira'd perched herself on a catwalk somewhere behind me, but she was keeping a close eye on things. I wasn't sure where Addie was, but I'd spotted her several times, fading in and out of the shadows, never in the same spot twice. Her job was to give the illusion of greater numbers, just in case Alberto thought shooting us and taking the loot was more cost-effective than writing an IOU.

"That's rude of him, seeing as I showed up in person. He implied I'd be shown the same courtesy."

I held out my palms in the universal sign for *What-can-you-do?* "What do you want, an apology? We've got business to discuss, limited-time offer. You gonna walk out 'cause my boss bruised your ego? Fine, but there's others in this city like you— but less sensitive. What'll it be?"

I already knew the answer. Alberto'd committed the moment he walked in, possibly since he'd first gotten the call. He was broke, and the other capos were smelling blood. He needed money, and fast—and was therefore in no position to snub rude business partners.

Not that I, a youthful gang recruit acting as a proxy, would know anything about that.

Alberto hemmed, hawed, made a big show of it, and—eventually—relented. "Alright. I'll stay. But I'm not in yet. Sell me."

Sure I would, up the river. But I kept that thought to myself and waved a hand. "Wallace! The goods!"

I heard scraping behind me, but I didn't turn away from Alberto, whose beady eyes were narrowed with interest. Finally, Z stepped into my field of vision, dragging one of the six crates behind him. He stopped between us, right in the center of the circle of dim light, and opened the crate. Alberto took a few steps forward, still cautious.

"You know what those are?" I asked.

Alberto closed the last few steps and stared into

the crate. His eyes widened. "Sniper rifles, by the look of it. A fine collection."

"What you're looking at is an M-twenty-four American sniper rifle," I said. Suddenly, Kira's voice, half-whispered, was in my ear and I repeated her words as fast as she said them. "Five-round magazine. Bolt-action. Twelve pounds. Eight-hundred-meter range. Twenty rounds per minute. Accurate. Dependable. Army standard until twenty-ten."

"How many crates?"

"Six," I said. There was more scraping as Z started bringing the other crates into the center. "Fifteen guns per crate."

It'd cost the last of mine and Kira's savings, but we'd managed the purchase (the others'd declined to contribute, and it's not like I could force them). Between the racehorse and the miniature armory, the CPC was running low on liquid assets. Our next move would have to make more money than it cost, because if recent trends continued, we'd be millions in the red before our vendetta against the mob was close to over.

"And you brought them here to show them off to me? Or . . . " Alberto's voice was drier than an Arizona sidewalk. It was fascinating to see the difference between his demeanor at the racetrack and his attitude here, in his capacity as capo.

"I'm glad you asked," I said, taking a step back, further into the shadows. "You know Mike Lolan?"

It was practically a rhetorical question. Mike Lolan was the top weapons dealer in the area, at least according to Z. Of course, Z also said they'd met at an upscale restaurant when Mike mistook him for a client and sat at his table. I wasn't sure I believed that, but it's not like I had evidence suggesting otherwise. Anyway, Mike had sold us the rifles, and he'd been nice enough to warn us that they were "hot" items, meaning the government wanted them back. We'd taken them despite the warning—well, *because* of it, but Mike didn't have to know that. He might've canceled our discount if he had, and that was the only thing keeping them affordable.

"Yeah, I know him."

"He gave us these beauties and a job. He's got a buyer in Jersey. Hired us to escort the M-twenty-fours down there and ensure everything goes—"

"Why didn't he use his own men?"

I held his gaze. "Busy month? Why ask *me*? He sure didn't tell me why."

Addie appeared again, this time from behind a row of shelving. She made fleeting eye contact with me—sending a tingle down my spine entirely unrelated to the cold—then ducked back behind it before Alberto or his men could notice she was the same person they'd been seeing all night.

"Long story short, we can't do the job anymore. But it still needs doing, or we don't get paid. That's where you come in."

"And you didn't ask Scipio because . . . "

According to our intel, Scipio was the capo in charge of illegal arms smuggling . . . and one of Alberto's rivals. Even if Z hadn't told me, I would've figured it out from Alberto's flash of bitterness as he said Scipio's name. Even in the dim light, it was easy to see.

"All due respect, sir, as he *is* a colleague of yours . . . " I demurred.

"Tell me."

"Well . . . my employer isn't impressed with his attention to detail. He wants this job done *right*."

Alberto's chest puffed with pride.

"We'd originally made the deal with Vito DiGiovanni, but his recent arrest complicated things. His wife recommended you to us as a resourceful, cunning, and influential man—not to mention good at managing your assets." I couldn't help it, I *had* to sneak in some dramatic irony where I could. It's practically a CPC tradition.

"A little *too* cunning," said Alberto. "There's a catch, or you'd deliver them yourself. What's wrong with these guns?" If he'd noticed my last remark, he didn't show it.

"The problem's on our end. Suffice it to say, the heat's too hot for us right now. You'll understand if I don't go into detail." I might've been fine telling him the truth, given his current financial situation, but lying was safer. I *was* expecting him to pry deeper, but he moved on without questioning the vagueness of my story.

"And if I *did* deliver these weapons, how would we be compensated?"

"Mike was gonna pay us thirty thousand. You can check that figure with him, if you like. You deliver the goods, ninety percent's yours."

"Ninety-five," said Alberto almost immediately.

I smiled, even though nobody else could see it. Alberto was in no position to negotiate, for all he was trying to hide it.

"I'm not here to haggle, Mr. Fettucci. Ninety percent."

He glared into the darkness at me and lifted his hand. The three men behind him pointed their guns at my chest. "And if I decide to take the weapons and go?"

I lifted my hands and clapped slowly. Each clap echoed hollowly in the warehouse. Mocking . . . and signaling.

"You know, Mr. Fettucci, I wondered if you were gonna try this route. I'm not armed, just as you demanded. But in the interest of fairness, you should know I lied about the number of guns in those crates. I said there were fifteen in each, as you'll recall. But in one, there are only fourteen."

Alberto chuckled. "A single gun makes for poor insurance."

"You misunderstand," I said. "Unit five. Demonstrate."

There was a *crack,* and the wood by Alberto's left foot shuddered and splintered. He hopped backwards and looked in shock at the large hole in the floor.

"Tell your men to stand down, Mr. Fettucci, or

the next one goes between your eyes. At this range, they won't have a head to bury you with."

"Stand down," said Alberto. He didn't sound angry in the slightest. One by one, his men pointed their weapons at the ground. "Well done. I was wondering if you'd be amateur enough for that to work."

"My boss doesn't hire amateurs, Alberto," I said, dropping his last name deliberately. "Do we have a deal?"

"We do."

Alberto extended a hand over the crates. I hesitated.

"Shake, or there's no deal."

"That important, huh?"

"You'd be surprised how honest a simple hand-shake makes some men."

If it had to be done . . . I gritted my teeth and stepped forward into the light. Step by step I approached the crates, willing any visible signs of discomfort away. My hand clasped his, and we shook. I stared at him defiantly, knowing my youth was all too apparent. Thankfully, he didn't comment on it.

"We'll give you the delivery address and the location of the last rifle once we're sure we aren't being tailed," I said, putting steel into my words.

Alberto sighed. "Only fair, I suppose."

He released the handshake and waved to his men, who holstered their weapons and began moving the crates. I retreated into the gloom . . . and just about jumped out of my skin as someone grabbed my hand.

It was Addie, of course. "Stop *doing* that," I growled.

She stuck out her tongue. "You know you like it," she said, giving my hand a squeeze. "Nice job."

"He was never *not* gonna take it," I said. "I just talked at him for a bit."

Hot tip—false modesty works wonders with the ladies.

We watched as one by one, the crates were

moved out the service door. When the last was gone, Alberto followed it. "Good doing business with you!" I called after him. He did not reply.

"You think he suspects anything?" asked Z from the shadows. All I could see of him were his eyes and teeth.

"He might," I said. "But his only choice is to risk it—without money, he can't fend off the other capos. We offered him his only escape, and he took it. Now we're gonna bar the door."

"Can I do it?" asked Z. I handed him a burner phone (suppressing an instinctive "*May* I"). The number was already entered—he just had to press *call*.

"Hello? Yeah, I'm reporting an unmarked black van on Bergen Street, heading west. They're carrying six crates of weapons stolen from the US Army . . . "

EIGHT

ENTIMETER BY CENTIMETER, THE MARKER DRAGGED across the whiteboard, leaving a thick line of red ink in its wake. With a flourish as I reached the end, I lowered it.

And the first capo on our list was crossed out.

"Pat yourselves on the back, guys," I said, stepping away from the wall. "You've earned it."

There was a scattering of applause. Weak applause, since only three people were clapping, but heartfelt and enthusiastic all the same.

"But from here, the game changes. We put one capo away, but he was an easy target. The rest—we dunno how many for sure—are all more popular than our friend Alberto. And now that one capo's down, the rest'll be on high alert. To cap it all off, I *may* have exhausted our assets getting this far."

Z nudged Kira. "By *may have*, he means he totally did."

"And it got results!" I said quickly, and maybe somewhat defensively. "Could we have gotten away with fewer guns, or a discount racehorse, or no racehorse at all? Perhaps. But the margin of error would've been unacceptably large. Money won't do us any good if we die before we spend it."

Due to the nature of ongoing campaigns, what *should've* been the Revel was bleeding into next plan's Frame. I'd make it up to the team with the mother of all parties once the Bonanno Family was broken beneath us.

"What's our war chest?" asked Addie quietly. Her head was cocked slightly, her eyes glazed over in thought. She'd barely spoken all meeting.

"Assuming I can sell the last M-twenty-four for as much as I paid? About nine thousand dollars plus whatever I can skim from Lucas . . . and any-thing you and Z wanna contribute."

I'd meant it as a joke, but it came out a little harsher than intended . . . and all the more con-demning for Kira's look of agreement.

"Um, sorry?" said Z, the tiniest bit of frost creeping into his voice. "We let you empty the war chest. Now you're mad because we kept our money?"

I gave Addie a surreptitious glance to see how she'd taken my comment, but it didn't look like she'd even noticed.

"Riiiight," said Kira. "You can't take a few K outta your *shampoo* budget—"

"Just a joke," I said quickly. "Z, it's fine. I never expected any help from you . . . or you either, Kira. Thanks for what you've lent me, it's helped. But if we're running low on cash, the answer isn't to squeeze you guys until you're broke. We need an Op that *makes* money instead of costing us. Now, I know what you're thinking—"

"You do?" asked Z.

"—You're thinking, it'll be tough enough *targeting* another capo now they're paranoid, much less parting them from their cash—"

"Not me." Z again.

"—And besides, who's to say they've got the money we need? That's why I'm proposing we skip the capos and move on to the street boss himself."

Again I looked at Addie, counting on her to say, "I agree," or, "Brilliant!" or, "Aha! That way, the capos struggle for power and do half our work for us in the ensuing chaos!" But she was looking past me, like something fascinating was written on the whiteboard. I checked. There wasn't.

"Addie, you with us?"

"Hmmm?" Hearing her name snapped Addie out of her trance. "Yeah, sorry. I just feel like shit today. Stomachache or something."

"Go see the nurse," said Kira.

"That's the plan. After the meeting."

But she sat up straighter, and her eyes were focused and aware.

"Anyway," I continued, "I don't have a plan for the boss yet. I'm hoping Z can chat up Vince a little, see what we can find. If we can't pull it off, I'll think of something else. But if we can cut the head off the power structure—"

"Won't work," said Z.

We all looked at him.

He sighed. "Am I the *only* one who actually researched this shit? The Mafia ain't a group of post-apocalyptic bandits. They're smart and organized. You jail a street boss, the underboss takes over the same day. No questions asked. They've got systems for all sorts of shit to keep everything running smoothly no matter what. You know, like *you* would if you ran a gang."

I wanted to defend myself, but he was right, I should've known this stuff. In my defense, I'd had a lot to learn and very little time to learn it.

"And it *works,*" said Z into the silence he'd

created. "The Bonannos've actually dealt with this kinda thing before. Joseph Massino, caught and convicted in two thousand five. Turned informant in jail. Gave them a real bad time. But leadership passed smoothly. Not even their boss ratting them out made the kind of chaos you're thinking of."

"Because they were united against a common enemy," I countered. "If we made it look like the underboss is *behind* the boss's downfall . . . "

Z shrugged. "You can try, but they've held on to power for a reason. They've got systems, backup plans. They're prepared for just about anything. We've been lucky so far, and it helps that they dunno who we are. But they're competent, dude. And dangerous."

I hadn't been expecting an argument with Z, of all people. He can be judgmental—of both me *and* my plans—but it's always quiet snark, not open disagreement.

Even more surprising, he'd *won*. Decisively.

There were two possibilities here. First, that

Z knew things would go *very* badly for us if we tried this plan. For some reason, he'd done lots of research, and was so confident in his knowledge that he was willing to argue vehemently against me, despite not being prone to doing so. Second, that Z'd been paid off by the Mafia (or had another ulterior motive) to discredit all my good ideas. While I wasn't dismissing the second possibility out of hand, the first seemed *much* likelier.

"Alright," I sighed. "It's obvious who's done his homework here. Got any ideas?"

"Hey, not my department," said Z. "I don't wanna leave you out in the cold, but I also don't wanna intrude on your turf . . . "

"Do you at least know who the street boss *is*? Did Vince let it slip?"

"I think so," said Z. "Some of Dad's friends were assigned to the Mafia once and they'd talk about it sometimes. I wasn't supposed to know, but," he grinned, "I'm pretty charming."

I'd forgotten Z's dad was a policeman. He'd

probably grown up hearing stories about the Mafia right from the front lines. Of *course* he'd know this stuff.

It made me feel a little better.

"I dunno if he's still in charge," said Z. "But the Bonanno street boss used to be a guy named Lorenzo Michaelis—*Il Diavoletto*, the mob called him. Slippery motherfucker, always one step ahead of the cops. They never got enough evidence to put him away—got close once, before three cops on the case died. All Dad's friends."

His smile had long since faded.

"He sounds dangerous," I said.

"This whole thing's dangerous."

Lucas's voice was echoing in my head again, but he was saying two things at once. In one breath he was counseling me to be prudent, avoid danger. In the other, he mocked my cowardice. *Without risk, nothing would ever get done. Do you want to accomplish nothing?*

At least this time, I knew he wasn't influencing my choice.

"If Lorenzo's still the street boss," I said, feeling the weight of the decision, "We take him down. If not, we find out who *is*."

The name *Lorenzo Michaelis* joined Alberto Fettucci's on the whiteboard. After a moment's hesitation, I circled it.

"So far, our tactics're working," I said, mostly to myself. Thinking out loud. "We figured out early that the NYPD was compromised, but that can only help the mob so much. If we lure them in and they get caught at a crime scene, all the leverage in the world won't help them."

I wrote *FRAME/SET UP → JAIL* in big block letters by Lorenzo's name.

"It's a simple plan, but they never see it coming," said Kira. "We've done it what, four times now?"

"Why change what works?" asked Addie. She sounded strained—the pain must've been worse than she was letting on.

"Ideally, we'd change things up right before they start catching on," I said. "The question is, has the time come?"

Z coughed. I tried to ignore him, but he coughed again, more insistently. He was *loving* being the resident expert for once.

"Do you have something to share with the class?"

"You got it," said Z. "Even if you have the perfect plan, jail might not hinder him too much. Historically, convicted mob bosses keep giving orders and running things from their cells, with the underboss serving as street boss and mouthpiece. Almost nothing actually changes. That always frustrated Dad."

I drew a big question mark beside *JAIL* and frowned at it. Maybe I should postpone the meeting until I'd brushed up on my Mafia history.

"We're also strapped for cash. If we go after *Lorenzo's* money . . . " I mused, and when Z didn't immediately shoot it down, I wrote *RUIN FINANCIALLY* under *JAIL?* and underlined it.

"Undermine him," said Addie softly. "Loyalty's one of their biggest strengths. We'll have to break that trust, or at least bend it out of shape. Especially between Lorenzo and his underboss, or the underboss and the capos. Make them doubt each other."

"You sure you're okay?" said Kira, concern written all over her face. "You sound awful."

"I told you, I'm fine," said Addie, but I could hear the pain behind her words. "Just a stomachache. The stomachache from hell. Like my stomach is a portal to hell and demons keep crawling out. But it'll pass. This one's just bad."

She shuddered, and I banished the urge to throw my arms around her back to the impetuous corner of my brain it'd come from. Instead I just said "Feel better. That's an order."

That got a smile out of her. "Sir, yes sir."

I put *UNDERMINE* on the list of ideas. "That about covers the basics, I think."

We looked at the board for a bit. Finally, Z spoke up again.

"If we got other families involved—"

"No," I said firmly. "That could easily become a full-blown disaster, and we'd have no control over it either way."

"You'll be involving them anyway. If we keep our victories going, they're gonna smell weakness and move in. You can't stop them."

"We'll deal with that when we have to," I said flatly. "I'm not gonna involve the gangs, just like I'm not gonna hire mercenaries to kill Lorenzo Michaelis."

"Jason—" said Addie.

"Why not?" asked Kira. She looked almost offended. "You mean because you'd ask *me*, right?"

"The moment the first body hits the ground, the stakes shoot sky-high," I said. "It's dangerous to take that step. But if I have no other choice—"

"How *pragmatic*," Z interrupted, incensed. "Isn't

'I don't wanna kill people' a good enough reason for you?"

"*Jason,*" said Addie again, this time firmly. Her tone said *stop talking* so I did. The room fell silent. And then she looked pointedly towards the doorway.

It was open. Someone was standing in it.

"Hi, Mr. Lister," Kira blurted awkwardly.

I lunged at the whiteboard, erasing long swaths of words with my shirtsleeve. But it was too late, I knew. He'd seen.

How long had he been there? How much had he heard?

"I'm not sure how to react," he finally said, in the calm measured voice I knew so well from AP English. "I still can't believe what I heard. Perhaps once I've accepted it, I'll know what's to be done with you. Where is your faculty sponsor?"

I couldn't help it. Neither could Kira or Z. Our heads swiveled towards Professor Gildfin like they were marionettes on the same string.

Mr. Lister's mouth narrowed.

"I see," he said sadly. "I think you'd better return to lunch now. When I've decided what I should do, I'll do it."

He stepped aside, leaving the doorway open. Slowly, sheepishly, we gathered our things.

"Mr. Lister—" Addie tried, but he shook his head before she could get past his name.

"I said, I'll decide what to do with you later."

He stood by the door until we'd all left. Then he shut it behind us and watched us trudge down the corridor towards our next class.

Whatever was coming next, it wouldn't be good.

NINE

"**M**EETINGS WITH OUR PARENTS," SAID KIRA venomously, glaring at everything within her field of vision and then some. "Won't that be a barrel of roses."

That could be a disaster for Kira. Her parents don't even know she likes fighting—they just think she's really into working out. The prospect of Mr. Appargus giving them some secondhand rendition of what Mr. Lister'd seen and heard was freaking her out, as evidenced by the small pile of shredded napkin by her plate.

"Just me, *Mamá,* and old Appargus," said Addie. She'd nestled into the crook of my arm, her cheek resting against my shoulder. "The subject? 'Your daughter is trying to rob, harm, or otherwise inconvenience a pillar of our community.'"

The Habana was a small, friendly, Cuban restaurant just off Madison Square. Since we couldn't meet in private at school now that Mr. Lister'd disbanded the CPC, we'd eaten here the past three nights. The food was passable, but the booths were cozy—and, more importantly, *private.*

"If Z hadn't mentioned starting a *gang war*—" I began.

"Sure, blame the black guy," said Z from across the table. He'd slouched against the wall like he wanted to merge with it. "Because you totally weren't talking about killing Lorenzo—"

"I was talking about *not* killing him! And getting the gangs involved wouldn't have killed anyone! Nope! Not a fucking soul!"

"People *die* in gang wars. They don't get premeditatedly murdered by teenagers. One's gonna stand out more than the other."

I took two deep breaths. I was better than petty fighting. *We* were better than petty fighting. We were in deep shit, and the way out was by working together, not tearing each other down.

"I'm not sure we should've dropped that idea so soon," said Kira thoughtfully.

"Forget the idea," I said before we could start arguing again. "Forget the whole *plan* for now. We need to survive these meetings first. He split us instead of having one big meeting, so he'll probably be comparing notes between us. We need a consistent story."

"A secret agent club?" Addie suggested. "It explains the secrecy—the CPC front, Professor Gildfin. We can say we were pretending Lorenzo was our 'Mission: Impossible,' so we were roleplaying how we might—"

"Roleplaying?" Kira gagged. "I thought we *didn't* want our parents to be ashamed of us."

Z laughed. Nobody joined him.

"Glad you've got my back," Kira said to him. "You're the only one who appreciates me."

She didn't notice the little glow of happiness Z was suddenly emitting, but I did.

"I'm just not in the mood for jokes," I said. "They suspend kids for *plastic knives* these days. There could be consequences. And if the teachers we've bribed start coming forward, well . . . I dunno how bad that could get, but at the very least, we could kiss college goodbye." I punctuated that last sentence with a large bite of steak sandwich.

"We want to be very nice and supportive of Mr. Lister, then," said Addie. "Teachers stick together when students attack them. If it looks like we're making trouble for him, other teachers will be incentivized to smear us."

I looked out the window at the fading afternoon sunlight and wondered how my parent-teacher meeting'd go. Would Lucas throw me under the bus? Clap me on the back and tell me I'd done well? Try and make me intern at his stupid hedge fund again? They were all equally likely. That man's unpredictability is near the top of a very long list of annoying things about him.

Z's phone rang, and he answered it immediately. On a bad day, this happens several times a meeting, and he *always* refuses to ignore his calls. We paused our conversation, resigned.

"Hey, man! What's up?"

I never heard what was up, but I *did* see Z's expression freeze over like he'd been dipped in liquid nitrogen.

"Thanks," he said in slow, carefully measured tones. "Listen. There's others, right? Yeah. Thought so. No, I wouldn't ask. You've done enough. Thanks. Bye."

He was breathing heavily, like the minute-long conversation'd been a full marathon. Lowering the phone slowly, he closed his eyes and said in that same protracted, careful voice, "They've put a hit on us."

"The mob?" I asked. Suddenly, my throat felt very dry. Z didn't answer, but he didn't need to.

"I didn't know he'd joined," he said, looking at his phone. "Haven't spoken in years. He heard Lorenzo give the order and called me straightaway. This literally just happened."

Somewhere out there, someone'd just been ordered to kill me. Possibly multiple someones. It should've been flattering—but it just *wasn't*.

My first thought was that we couldn't go home for a while, but I saw the flaw there almost immediately—the Mafia didn't know where we were. So they'd check our houses first.

"Holy shit," whispered Z. "Our parents."

Kira went white and her cup shattered in her hand, sending glass shards and ice spilling across her lap.

A vein pulsed in Addie's neck, the only movement she'd made since Z'd made his pronouncement. But the tinkling of glass hitting the floor snapped her out of her reverie. "When?" she whispered, and I could tell she was afraid of the answer.

Z hesitated. "Tonight," he said. "But later. Not now."

"We have time, then," I said, trying to inject some calm into the situation. I was mentally better off than the others by far, probably because the idea of assassins penetrating Lucas's security was as ludicrous as Z skipping his shower.

"I see two options," I said. "We can evacuate our families, or spread the word that we're elsewhere. Or turn ourselves in . . . three options. But I don't like that one."

Problem was, I didn't like the others either. They just delayed the inevitable—the Mafia wouldn't cancel a hit because the target's house was empty. One way or another, we'd have to reckon with them . . . or spend all our lives on the run.

I needed to think. No, I needed *time* to think. "Gimme ten on a timer."

"Just call the fucking cops," said Kira hoarsely. "They'll—"

"Ten minutes. Please."

Kira fell silent, which I appreciated. When the boss asks for ten minutes, you give him ten minutes. Z and Addie seemed to realize this too—they stayed quiet and watched me, calmer than they had any right to be. Probably because we had some time. Not much . . . but *at least* ten minutes.

The next ten minutes were among the tensest of my life. Every so often, I'd ask Z about each hit squad's numbers, weapons, tactics, et cetera. To each question, Z'd say he didn't know. And my planning capability would be constrained that much more.

Kira began pushing cup debris off her lap with mechanical motions and a blank expression. I told myself to breathe regularly and deeply. Breathing was important. In, out. Take in all information, filter out everything extraneous. Rearrange what's left into something, *anything* coherent . . .

The timer on Z's phone beeped and the group looked at me expectantly.

"Here goes," I said, pressing down on the table

with my hands. "Long-term, the best solution's hiring mercenaries to guard our parents surreptitiously twenty-four/seven. Obviously, that isn't feasible short-term, as hiring a mercenary takes longer than we currently have."

Kira made an impatient noise.

"Yes, well. Short-term, I have bad news. We can't call the cops. Remember, we know the NYPD's been infiltrated. If we call in, there's a chance the Mafia gets tipped off. Then they'll just accelerate the schedule and target our houses before the cops can respond. That's not guaranteed, but I'm not comfortable taking the risk. And like most plans I thought about, it doesn't actually *help*. At best, the Mafia retreats, makes a better plan, and bumps us off when we least expect it. Only this time, they'll know we know they're coming. And account for it."

I leaned in conspiratorially. "No, *now's* the best time to stop them, while still have the advantage of surprise. And since we can't trust law enforcement, the task falls to us."

Everyone looked at me like I'd bought a ticket to Crazytown. I ignored them—there's a fine line between genius and insanity, but I'm well on the safe side.

"We go home *now*. Call ahead and make our families leave somehow, out of the line of fire. Whatever crazy excuse you need, just get them out. *That's* when we call the NYPD. Best-case scenario, the cops arrive and help us prepare. Worst-case, they tip off the mob, who send their squads. But here's the thing—they'll have to move in before they're ready. Under-equipped, without a plan, maybe missing key members. The less time we give them to prepare, the less dangerous they'll be."

"Still plenty dangerous," said Addie. I had to admit, she had a point.

"Hold up," said Z. "Why would the cops sell us out?" He looked almost hurt.

Right. Z *would* take the notion personally that his dad's friends—or even his dad—might be corrupt.

"They might not," I said. "That'd be great. But if they *don't*, the mob'll arrive after the cops, and there could be a firefight. That possibility puts police lives at stake. And cops stand together, even sometimes against the people they've sworn to protect. You know that."

Z glared, but didn't say anything. I'd sandwiched him between his heritage and his father.

"There's good cops," I told him, softening. "Your dad's one. But there's also crooked cops, and they can justify selling out some civilians—"

"Argue about this later," said Kira through gritted teeth. She was shredding her napkin again.

"Right. Well, the mob shows up, disorganized, trying to beat the police dispatch that's coming. And run smack into *us*."

"And shoot us dead. You think us four can handle a team of hit men?" snapped Z.

"Actually . . . they're gonna send four teams simultaneously, probably. So we'll have to split up. One per team."

Z slumped back, shaking his head. "Great. We're dead."

"I'm thinking we'll secure our own houses, since we know them best," I said, ignoring Z. "We have a little time, but the faster we get moving, the less time they get. So we should move. *Now.*"

Nobody moved.

"*Mamá* doesn't have a phone," muttered Addie. "Can't warn her."

"You'll have to tell her in person, then," I said. "Guys, it's not that bad. I've already got a basic plan. Remember, we don't have to fight them off single-handedly, just delay them until the cops arrive. But we *have to go.*"

"I . . . " Kira looked at me intensely. I could feel the fear behind her eyes, but I couldn't tell what she was trying to communicate, and she seemed to've been incapacitated by a bout of shyness. Which wasn't like Kira at all.

But that's not quite true. I'd seen her like this before. In Mandalay Bay, before lunch. During the conversation that'd led me to suspect Kira was running away from fights. That she was worried about what her adrenaline addiction was doing to her.

"My parents, I don't . . . If they see me fight, they . . . " Kira looked at the floor evasively.

That was another thing. Kira's always been sensitive about how her family sees her. She's their perfect first child—a pretty, popular, multi-talented senior with good prospects. And she'll guard that facade with her life. Maybe even literally.

I imagined Kira shot by mobsters, unwilling to lift a finger in her own defense because her family was watching.

"Switch with me?" asked Kira, looking pleadingly at Addie.

Addie looked at her, then took her hand and shook it. "Yeah. I . . . I trust you. You can trust me, too. I won't let anyone touch them."

Kira said nothing, but she had gratitude written in bold across her face.

I stood, hoping the others would follow this time. Surprisingly, they did—even Z. "I can't believe we're doing this," he groused. "It's insane."

"A little," I agreed. "But there's no better way." At least, not one I'd seen. But I'd thought for ten minutes, and for thinking purposes, ten minutes is as good as ten hours. I *had* to believe in this plan, because there was no time to second-guess myself.

"How do we get there?" asked Addie. "We've only got two cars."

"You and Kira take hers, she'll drop you off on the way. Z and I take his. I'll call a cab to wait at his house, and take it to mine. That'll be fastest."

"I'll take your word for it," said Addie. "Alright. Be careful." She leaned in and gave me a quick kiss on the cheek. "If you die, I'll never forgive you."

"You too," I said.

You too. How easily my wit crumbled in Addie's presence. But there was something different about this time. Maybe it was the possibility that I'd never see her again, or maybe just the kiss, but I *refused* to leave things like that.

So I tried again. "Addie, I, well . . . "

All my eloquence evaporated faced with those green eyes.

"You should know, in case something happens . . . "

My tongue was a limp, dry knot. Addie waited, expectant, as I worked it back and forth.

"I . . . "

"I *do* know," she said after waiting on me for precious seconds. "Let's talk later. No time right now."

The moment awkward emotions left the mix, my brain snapped back into full working order.

"Right. I can explain the plan over the phone as we drive."

"Good thinking," said Addie. "Save us some time. Alright, well . . . Let's go, Kira."

"Good luck," I said to her retreating back, unable to look away from the girl I was crazy about, the girl I was sending into the path of an assassination. If something went wrong and she . . . well, if something went wrong, I'd live with that forever. Addie was . . . well, amazing in her role, but she was no fighter. Not like Kira.

Though, now that I remembered . . . "Hey Kira, hold up."

Kira looked at me curiously, but trotted over. I put my hand on her shoulder and guided her into a corner. "What?" she said suspiciously.

I tilted my head up and looked her right in the eye. "No bullshit. You gonna fight?"

I had to know. *Had to.* For Addie's mom's sake.

"You *did* notice." Her tone was flat. "Should've figured."

"Hard not to," I pointed out, refusing to break eye contact.

Finally, Kira's expression hardened in determination. "Yeah. I'll fight. Don't worry about it."

I gave her shoulder a reassuring squeeze. "I'm not."

I was, though—deathly worried. Kira was just . . . well, a kid. We all were. What could we *do* against a team of hardened killers?

But there was another, more important question. What choice had we but to try?

I motioned to Z, then jerked my head toward the restaurant exit. He caught up with long strides and we left together, with Addie and Kira following close behind.

The Havana had its own lot, but Z'd parked on the street. He hit the unlock button on his keys and threw open the door. I took one last look at Kira and Addie as they turned into the lot, hoping I hadn't just sentenced them to death.

Then I got in. Z was already behind the wheel, tapping his foot impatiently. Before I could close the door, he twisted the keys.

The passenger door slammed shut and the engine roared to life.

TEN

'D HAD LIMITED TIME TO CONSTRUCT THREE SEPARATE family-saving plans, tailored to each household. They *obviously* had shortcomings, but had turned out quite well given the circumstances. Z didn't see it that way.

"If I weren't driving, I'd beat your ass," he said after I'd explained his.

"It'll work," I protested. "You can't—"

"Sure I can," said Z. "The others ain't like that. I *heard* them."

Anger rolled off him like a storm cloud. He'd spent most of the drive angry, actually. But explaining the plan had strengthened it.

"Addie's in mortal danger," I said patiently. "Kira's in mortal danger. All the plans involve it."

"Yeah, but this ain't *me*," snapped Z. "It's my family. We wanna save them, not—"

"You wanna put yourself in danger?" I said, voice rising slightly. "That's fair, I guess—the girls are. What can you do, Z? What can you contribute that both stops the attack and shifts the danger to you? Get the neighbors to form an arm-link chain around the house? Ask the neighborhood ice cream man for help? *Someone's* gotta be *in danger*, and your dad has officer training! Involving him mitigates the risk of someone dying tremendously!"

Z took a few deep breaths. "I get it. I'm a useless son-of-a-bitch."

"Hey, no one invited you to a pity party. But this is your dad's *job*. And he's good at it. He'll be fine."

"Uh-huh. But Mom and my siblings, why can't *they* go?"

"I guess they can," I conceded. "But if you explain why they have to leave, they won't let *him* stay."

"Then you'd better hope I explain things *really well*." said Z caustically, and raised his phone to his ear (Yeah, yeah, unsafe driving habits, save it for someone who cares). "Dad," he said into the speaker, enunciating clearly.

The sun was sinking towards the horizon, lengthening shadows and lighting the sky a patchy lavender. Real dusk was still a half-hour away, which meant if we stayed on schedule, the mob would be attacking in light. That wouldn't singlehandedly turn the tide, but no advantage was too small to scrounge for. The margin of error was *that* thin.

And even a perfect plan was guesswork when *guns* entered the equation. A single lucky shot, no matter how unlikely, could mean failure. And failure could mean death. And death could mean . . . well, I didn't wanna discover what death could mean.

"Hey," said Z into the phone. "I got some bad news. Well, that's underselling it. The—well, the house is gonna be attacked."

I mouthed "*Speaker phone*," but he ignored me.

Maybe because he was looking at the road instead of my lips. Probably not.

"The Mafia. Yeah. Don't ask me how I know. A friend, okay? I can't—it ain't important."

Z paused for breath and I hissed, "*Speaker phone,*" loud enough that he could hear. Yes, definitely ignoring me.

"I dunno, Dad," he said, exasperated. "Maybe they think you're trying to put them away. Not important. You guys gotta go."

"*Z,*" I growled. It *wasn't the time* to pull this shit. At least he had the courtesy to look guilty.

"You got some time," he said. "Maybe fifteen minutes."

Z scoffs at my plans a lot, but when push comes to shove, he always follows orders. Always *did*, at least. We had an understanding, I'd thought, that if he wanted to change a plan on me, I'd need enough time to compensate for that.

He'd given me remarkably little time to compensate for *this*.

"What?" said Z sharply. "No, Dad. No. You too."

I needed to hear their conversation. Grabbing the phone seemed guaranteed to end badly while Z was driving, and precision-stabbing the speaker phone button was past my pay grade. Were there any other options?

"It doesn't matter! No, I get it, but it's too dangerous. Dad—"

Wait. Newer cars had a built-in speaker system that coordinated with Smartphones automatically, right? I swear I'd seen Jeeves use it. His car had a similar touch interface to Z's. I tapped the screen experimentally. One of the menu tabs said *Wireless Functions*.

Worth a shot, right?

" . . .Won't arrive in time," said Z angrily. I stifled a smile. Z's dad obviously liked my plan better than his.

Near the screen's bottom edge was a phone icon radiating lines. I touched it, fingers crossed.

"*—Much earlier than fifteen minutes,*" said a low baritone voice. "*I'll call it in.*"

Z jumped as his father's voice filled the car.

"Don't do that," I said before he recovered. "I've got a plan, and it's important to not call before—"

"*Who's that?*"

"Dammit Jason—"

"*—We're ready. Mr., uh, Mr. Z's dad, can the house be fortified?*"

"*There're a few places,*" he replied, sounding a little confused. "*I'd want another couple bodies—*"

"You'll have them," I said. Z's hand shot towards the touch screen, scrabbling to deactivate the speaker, but I caught it and held it firmly. "Make what preparations you can and evacuate your family. We'll be there shortly."

"No, Dad, go with them. You don't gotta—"

"He wants to," I said. "Now remember, don't call the cops. It could upset the plan if—"

"*Why not?*" said the voice. "*Hell, why should I trust you?*"

As much as I wanted to, I couldn't deny the wisdom in that. I wouldn't have trusted me either.

"He's right, Dad," said Z. "This time, anyway."

"*Who* is *he?*" Z's dad sounded almost resigned. "*Another friend from school?*"

I cleared my throat to reply, but before I could, he continued. "*I hope it wasn't too important, because Marta just got off the phone with the police.*"

Great. Just fucking great.

Z wore a look of horror I suspected my own face was mirroring perfectly. But we couldn't afford the luxury of freaking out. It wasn't *necessarily* a catastrophe. Best-case scenario, the Mafia wouldn't be notified, the police would arrive with time to spare, and everything would be happily ever after.

Worst-case scenario, the Mafia'd be tipped off prematurely, with us still out of position and unprepared.

"It was," I said in my calmest voice. "We'll get back to you. We have some urgent calls to make."

"Bye, Dad," said Z and hung up, too worried to

be mad. The engine revved and the car accelerated again, doing a death-defying forty through the suburban streets.

Addie picked up in three rings. "Something wrong?"

"The cops were called," I said, speaking as quickly as possible. "Not by us. If they have an inside man, they know we know. Get in position. *Fast.*"

"Jesus," she said. "Kira just dropped me off. You need to tell her."

"Call Kira," I said to Z, and he lifted his phone again. "Kira Applewood," he said in that same, overly-enunciating voice.

"I should go," said Addie reluctantly. "Lots to do. Kira got her family out, so that's something."

"Good luck," I said, and hung up.

I let out a long breath, hoping I hadn't wasted my last words to Addie on *good luck*. Actually, that was probably tempting the gods of irony a little *too* heavily. I considered calling back to say something else, but the laws of narrative causality wouldn't *actually* save her, while an extra thirty seconds of prep time not wasted talking to me very well might.

Z hung up, and I wondered how best to inform him that this latest wrinkle was all his fault. If he'd just let *me* talk, I would've explained the whole plan first thing—but calmly and quietly, without his family listening in. Then we'd all have been on the same page, and voila, no added risk.

Z'd also tried to derail the plan itself. That, I couldn't let slide. But he beat me to the punch.

"You haven't called a taxi yet."

"What?"

"The taxi. To get to your place."

"Right."

I let the matter drop, leaving the car in uncomfortable silence.

"Only there ain't much time, and I ain't driving you," said Z, exasperated. "So if you're gonna call, you gotta—oh, hell."

Z actually turned in his seat, eyes off the road. I looked back, not even trying to deny it. I'd known it'd come to this eventually. I was surprised it'd taken him this long to work out.

"You aren't gonna do it," said Z. It was a statement, not a question.

"Luc—*Dad* has his own security team," I said. "State-of-the-art cameras, armed guards, motion sensors. You'll need me more than he will."

It wasn't technically a lie, but it was a poor excuse for the truth, and we both knew it. But he'd turned back to the road, and I couldn't see his face.

He gave me one more out—more generosity than I deserved. "You gonna call him, at least? Let him know what's coming?"

My non-response was the most telling answer I could've given.

Z sighed. "Cold, dude," he said at last. It wasn't a surprise. I knew he'd judge me.

You probably are too.

I'd probably feel differently if there was any chance the hit'd succeed. Honestly, I'd bet even money on them just *scrapping* the mission upon seeing the guards. And if they somehow made it through them to *Lucas*, well . . . it'd be *them* I felt sorry for.

We spent the rest of the ride in silence, on opposite sides of an ideological gulf too wide for words to cross. After what felt like an eternity of awkwardness (but according to my phone was just eight minutes) Z pulled up by a quiet, white-painted house with a modest yard.

"Go," he said, and I jumped out before he'd had time to shift into park. I darted up the walkway and stairs and knocked loudly.

The door opened, and I found myself looking down the twin barrels of a shotgun.

"Jason Jorgensen, nice to meet you," I said on autopilot. "Um . . . Z's right behind me."

Z chose that moment to emerge from the car.

The broad-shouldered black man in full police uniform behind the shotgun slowly lowered it. "Dammit," he said. "You guys came. Get outta here."

"Mom and the rest?" said Z, pushing the door open and dragging us indoors.

"Got them out," said Z's dad (I really needed a name). "All except Casey, she's got a playdate at the Duvalles'."

I looked around the antechamber as Z pulled the door shut behind us. There were some desks stacked near the far wall, behind a table turned on its side. I nodded my approval. "Nice barricade, Mr. . . . "

"Call me Hector," said Z's dad. "Where's my backup?"

"At your service," I said with a small bow.

"Like hell you are," said Hector, after he'd decided I wasn't joking. "You're still in school. And I'll take my chances alone before I put you in danger," he said to Z, who'd been about to argue.

Z fell silent—and shutting him up isn't easy. I *had* to learn that trick.

"No backup," Hector mused, looking around the room. "And they could come from anywhere. How much time we got?"

Not enough, thanks to you, I wanted to say, but curbed the impulse. "Any minute now."

"I can't fucking believe this," said Hector. "Coming here. You're a liability."

"Don't think of us like that." I looked to Z for backup, but he avoided my eyes. "We can help. We could mean the difference between—"

"Ever shot a gun?"

I was forced to admit I hadn't. Hector shook his head dismissively.

"Basement," he growled. "Both of you. Don't even *think* about leaving until it's over."

"But Dad, what if you—"

"I *said*, don't even think about it."

I resolved to involve myself the moment I found an opportunity.

"C'mon," muttered Z, leading me by the arm.

We passed several more makeshift barricades along the way—Hector'd used his warning well. I counted three before coming to a small staircase outside the kitchen. Down the steps we went, twisting back and around again until I found myself in a pitch-dark room.

"One sec," said Z. I heard him fumbling, and then the light flicked on.

It was a small, stone room with many shelves, all filled with cardboard boxes and plastic containers. By the far wall, some of these containers were stacked strategically, creating yet another barricade. Z and I looked at each other, then stepped behind it and sat. It covered our whole bodies as long as we stayed sitting.

"You know I'll never forgive you if this goes wrong, right?" said Z. It was our usual pre-job banter, but it didn't sound lighthearted—in fact, he looked deadly serious.

"Relax," I said. "It'll be fine. The plan's good."

At that moment, I heard a loud crashing sound, like glass and wood breaking at once. Then, the shooting began.

ADDIE

THE STEM RESISTED AT FIRST, BUT AS I CONTINUED pulling, its roots gave way centimeter by centimeter. Finally, with a plaintive *snap*, it slid free. I tossed it aside onto a growing pile of weeds.

I was adequately compartmentalizing and isolating my fear that Kira would call to report that she'd been too late, that *Mamá* was dead. My fear that I'd die heading off the attack on *her* family had been similarly dealt with. Pablo Flores had no reason to hold such fears, and therefore, I'd put them aside.

Pablo Flores, I'd decided, was twenty-three and inquisitive by nature, always getting into other people's business. He'd married for love just out of high school and given up his dreams of college to support his wife and—soon after—his daughter. His wife worked retail at American Eagle part-time while he worked in the suburbs as a gardener for upper middle class New Yorkers who wanted pristine lawns. He'd learned gardening from his *mamá*, whose garden had been the hobby she poured all her creative energies into every night after work. From Pablo's—*my*—standpoint, he was carrying on a family legacy of sorts, which helped him cope with the drudgery.

The straw hat I was currently wearing to keep the sun off my face (and obscure it somewhat) had been a fifteenth birthday present. It was small for his head, but he wore it anyway—it had sentimental value. My hair was still short enough for a boy's, so it hadn't needed to be tucked.

I hummed a content little tune as I worked, turning over the soil to find weed seeds I'd missed on my first pass. A patient mind and a thorough hand were vital to good gardening.

The trick to acting is to *be* the character. At least, that's how *I* do it. All the thoughts that make up Addie get wrapped into a little ball and shoved into the farthest corner of my brain for a while, and a whole new set take charge. As you might imagine, this can be difficult when your brain *really* wants to think about something. Like that your *mamá* is in mortal danger and you're sitting on a front lawn gardening.

At least Kira's family wasn't home anymore. Before we split off, she'd convinced them she was waiting at the mall with a surprise for them. The flaw there was that she *wasn't* at the mall, and *didn't* have any such surprise, but Kira could deal with a little social fallout from her family if it saved their lives.

I'd trust her with *my* life any day, so it should have been easy to trust her with *Mamá*'s, but it wasn't quite the same for irrational reasons my brain couldn't discard. And it isn't easy holding two people inside your headspace simultaneously at the best of times, much less when one is confronting her own mortality (not to mention her family's and friends') and the other is happy, carefree, passing the hours of work with a song and a smile.

If I could start again, I'd construct Pablo Flores a little differently. Make him more of a worrywart, maybe—just give him *some* way of feeding on Addie's emotions to achieve three-dimensionality. And I'd give him a less fitting last name. Real people don't follow apt naming schemas. Usually.

Worrying about Pablo's believability wouldn't make him any more believable. Not for the first time—though hopefully for the last—I envisioned myself smashing all my Addie-thoughts into a more compact, manageable size and tucking them away beneath my consciousness. Now, with an emptier mind, Pablo could emerge more fully, to enact his mannerisms within my body as well as my thoughts. My back, shoulders, and neck hunched and stooped, a result of long hours Pablo had spent on his knees contemplating the dirt he tended. My balance shifted down and back, towards my center. My eyes roamed eagerly about the street, searching for friends, whether established or potential.

I found them in the form of a chrome minivan that pulled up in front of my lawn. The engine stopped and three men, well-dressed and grim-faced, piled out. Their coats bulged oddly, but Pablo wouldn't notice that kind of thing—he was focused on the ground. Still, I gave them a happy smile and a wave as they walked up the Applewood residence's red-painted concrete walkway. They gave me searching gazes (giving me the familiar tingling sensation I get when someone's watching me) but didn't hesitate in their stride. Pablo didn't mind. Some people didn't believe in making friends. Besides, these men looked busy. They were probably important men, especially dressed like that.

Addie knew them for who they were, and wanted

to run, or at least glare. But I kept her hatred, her fear, locked up tight.

It gets easier every time.

I heard a loud thump and glanced up from the garden bed again, feeling a stab of legitimate annoyance. One of the well-dressed callers had knocked. After several long moments in which nobody answered, he knocked again.

"Hey!" I called in Pablo's voice, which was an octave deeper and more accented than Addie's—Northern Mexican, to be precise, with slight influence from San Diego, where Pablo had spent his first three years in America. Voice is incredibly important to a character's believability, and almost as unique as a fingerprint. My ears are always open to the speech of everyone around me, absorbing their cultural markers and linguistic quirks for repurposing later. "You looking for the Applewoods?"

As I spoke, my bubble of sound expanded rapidly, far past my call's intended targets. I was trying to ignore it—Pablo wouldn't see one, after all—but it wasn't something I could just *stop visualizing*. The best I could do was act like I didn't possess the additional information.

I can't remember how old I was when I realized not *everyone* had their own bubbles, but it took me longer than it should have.

The men seemed unsure how to respond, which Pablo found strange. Finally, one stepped forward. There was a strut to it—exaggerated arrogance to compensate for his stature, perhaps? Pablo wouldn't pick up on that, but Addie did.

"Yeah, we looking for 'em," he said. Pretty even mix between Italian-American and pure, unfiltered Boston, with the harsh twang of a man who chews his words before spitting them out. "We're their legal team."

Pablo felt a wrinkle of disquiet. "Anyone in trouble?" Pablo was concerned for his employers (who'd always treated him well), but *more* concerned for his employment prospects should they encounter hardships.

"Not if we do our job," he said. His words were oilier now, like he'd taken on the role of a stereotypical lawyer. Beneath the Pablo-mind, I felt respect for this man's skill . . . though it's generally better to stay away from stereotypes. It helps your character feel more real and actualized.

But that's hardly an amateur's mistake. Even the best actors sometimes fall into that trap.

"Well, they just left," I said. "In a damned hurry, they were. Almost forgot to pay me, but I reminded 'em."

The men on the porch exchanged glances.

"That's not good," said the short one. "You know where? It's an emergency," he added quickly.

I shrugged. "They don't tell me nothing. But they were carrying bags, suitcases. Prolly a vacation."

The short man frowned in consternation and turned to the slick-voiced lawyer, whose ruddy face was a mask of disappointment. But Pablo was nothing if not genuinely helpful. "If you want, you can gimme a message and next time I see 'em—"

"When did they leave?" interrupted the third man.

I shrugged again. I'd discovered that Pablo liked shrugging. "Who knows? I got here at noon, so . . . after then? Sorry. Time passes quick when you're gardening. You guys got gardens?"

I noticed the man who'd spoken last perk up at that. Pablo wouldn't have, but I made a judgment call and overrode his character momentarily. "Yeah?" I pointed at him. "What you got?"

He looked at me straight-faced. Trying to pretend he didn't have a garden. Too bad I knew better.

"Any carrots?" I asked, smiling warmly. It took all my Pablo-mind to make the smile genuine. "Got a crop at home. Picked some babies yesterday. Course, the Applewoods don't grow fruits and veggies. They don't like nothing but flowers."

"Carrots? Of course!" said the closet gardener, and his friends glared at him. I grinned reassuringly and he continued. "I'm a vegetable man, when I have the space. Carrots're nice and easy, so I've just about always got some growing." His voice was almost full New Yorker, with the faintest hint of Italian, but his hands were still as expressive as a native's.

"Yeah, carrots're the best," I said. "You ever come to the Farmer's Market?"

"Which?" He took a few eager steps towards me, falling naturally into the conversation while his friends fumed ineffectually. Perfect.

"Union Square?"

"Sure do. You?"

"Been thinking 'bout selling," I said with a shy smile. "But you need bulk. That's tough with a tiny little garden plot."

We swapped gardening stories as the men on the porch grew ever more impatient. One began speaking rapidly into a cell phone in Italian, but when he hung up, Orsino—my new friend—and I were still chatting. In fact, we'd just started a vigorous friendly debate about how to get larger tomatoes.

"Orsino," said the short one, who I'd decided

was calling the shots and had therefore nicknamed Napoleon, "we should go."

"Just a moment," said Orsino, waving him away. "But it doesn't make the tomatoes grainy? Bigger, yes, but the taste—ruined."

"You fix the taste by—"

"*Basta!*" snapped Napoleon, and then he let loose with an Italian litany that I *maybe* could have understood if the words hadn't blended together. I know a little Italian, but I'm no native speaker. One day, I'll rectify that.

Orsino sighed. "He's right. Nice meeting you, Pablo, but—"

"Wait," I said quickly. I had to keep stalling. "Gimme your phone. I'll text you."

Orsino reached into his pocket, but Napoleon grabbed his arm. "Don't—"

"Shove it up your ass," said Orsino, handing me his phone. "What're you afraid of?"

This prompted another rant in Italian, no doubt laced with plenty of invectives. Meanwhile, I put my number—well, Pablo's number, not *mine*—into the phone. I took my sweet time too, as much as I thought I could get away with.

It was tempting to open his messages and/or contacts and do some snooping. I've got the best memory of anyone I know, so it would have been just like taking a picture. But it wasn't worth the risk of someone noticing. I didn't have to do a risk/reward calculation to solve *that* one.

If Jason were in my position, maybe he'd have found a way. But then, he wouldn't have gotten this far in the first place.

"Alright," I said when I was sure I couldn't delay any longer. "You text that number, yeah? Pablo Flores. Actually . . . I'll do it right now."

"No, that's fine," said Orsino with a quick look at Napoleon, whose face was turning a mottled red. "I can handle it. Well . . . nice meeting you, Pablo."

I handed the phone back reluctantly. "You too—"

There it was, finally, as unmistakable as it was

overdue. Sirens, faint with distance, but getting louder by the second.

Pablo wasn't sure what to make of this, but he hoped the disturbance wasn't anywhere nearby. And that nobody he knew was involved.

The blood drained from Napoleon's reddening face, leaving an odd waxy parchment color behind, and Orsino's easy smile dissolved into fright.

They bolted to the van as one, but the third member was still on the porch, and as he ran by me, I stuck out my foot and tripped him. He hit the ground with a metallic crunch.

He leaped up angrily, murder in his eyes, but as I balled up my fists and squared my shoulders, he made a snap decision and ran for the van. He wanted to punish me for tripping him, but not as badly as he wanted to escape jail time. And he knew every second was precious.

They didn't get halfway down the street before a black armored car bristling with antennae and sporting a flashing siren array skidded to a stop in the middle of the road, blocking their exit. It was followed by two standard police cars, and then another from the other direction, closing off the street. The hit men had no real options but surrendering or opening fire.

They chose surrender pretty fast.

I dissolved the identity of Pablo Flores, letting him scatter into the recesses of my brain until he was needed again, and Addie took over. A job well done.

With the re-assumption of my Addie-self came a twinge of guilt for betraying Orsino—I always got that when I befriended a target. But I saw it like this—he'd tried to kill my friend's parents and sisters, which was orders of magnitude worse.

And besides, from a semantic standpoint, the friend he'd made wasn't me. That friend didn't even exist anymore.

KIRA

MY BLOOD WAS ITCHING, FIZZING LIKE A CAN OF root beer shaken past its breaking point. Like it didn't even need to be popped open, all that fizzing'd rupture the can and send the soda flying across the room. In this metaphor, I'm the can. And I'm seconds away from exploding.

Fuck it. Just fuck it. You do what you can, y'know? You learn to live knowing you're not normal, that fighting makes you hot, that you can't feel the pain of the people you hurt. You come up with all kinds of tricks to keep the tendrils of rage from dragging your brain down, like closing your eyes and imagining the anger drain out through your toes. And when that doesn't help, blasting heavy metal loud enough to drown out the urge to fight, injure, kill if possible.

Never done that, thank God. Yet.

You weasel your way outta the tasks you've built your rep around. You keep fights short and infrequent. You drop hints to your friends that maybe you wanna sit back, do some computer shit. Subtle hints, because you don't want them figuring out what's wrong with you, but hints all the same.

And then you learn the Mafia's sending people after your family and your friends' families, and that all goes to hell.

Because there was never any question of chickening out, not this time. Addie'd trusted me with her mom's life and fuck me if I was gonna let her down.

I was speeding. I usually am. It's kinda my natural state. When I put the pedal to the metal, I can leave the anger behind, outrun it. It catches up when I brake, but for a bit, I'm free. But this time, that wasn't the reason. This time, I was speeding because if I didn't, I could arrive too late. But as fast as I was going, I only had one eye to spare for the road. The other eye was glued to my cop-tracking app because the last thing I needed was to be pulled over.

I'd thought about letting that happen, explaining why I was speeding, and letting the cops take over. But if they didn't believe me, or even if they did but took too long calling it in and recording my info and jerking off, or whatever they're doing while you wait in your car, that path led to death too. I had a fantasy of speeding past a cop, then dodging him long enough to lead him to the Bristol household, but that'd actually just get me swarmed.

Nah, it was up to me. But I was cool with that because let's be real, I'm the toughest bitch around.

Squealing tires, angry honks, death metal, and beneath it all, the constant, reassuring throb of the engine. That was my jam. I felt that old familiar tingle in my knuckles, the kind that precedes a fight. That part of me the thrill comes from was aching for it, *singing* in anticipation, even while the rest of me tried to shut it down.

Sirens in the distance. Someone'd probably called about my driving. Or multiple someones. Well, only one way to deal with that shit. I pressed the pedal harder and shot forward like an arrow.

Remember, if you're going fast enough, they can't read your plates.

I aimed for the more deserted streets, which I

should've done from the start. The fewer people to call in my location and help the cops form a trail, the better. I blasted right through a stop sign, heard the horn and the sound of squealing brakes, and gritted my teeth for the crash. It didn't come, and I didn't spare a glance behind me to see how close I'd come. The close shave sent joyful tingles down my spine.

The GPS said four minutes. I did it in two. Through a residential area.

I skidded to a stop against the curb and sprang out, leaving the engine smoking. Double-checked the address. Yeah, this was it. But was I in time?

Only one way to find out.

I went around the side, opened the little wooden gate. I'm no Addie, but I tried to move as quiet as I could, keep my head down. Just in case. The garden was overrun by weeds and lemon-clovers. Everything seemed quiet. That was either good, or really, really bad.

Part of me, the part that sucks, was hoping I was

too late, that I wouldn't have to surrender to the song of battle inside me. Every time I do, it gets a little stronger. One day, it won't let me go.

That scares me more than any fight I've ever been in.

I eased open a window. Then, bracing myself for what I might find inside, I hurled myself through the hole I'd made.

Picked myself up. Some noise there, but nobody came running. Wondered idly if anyone was home. Car in the driveway, Addie didn't drive, it was just her and her mom at home. So probably.

Felt the battle-lust rising, sharpening my perspective. Cutting out extraneous information. Doorways I took note of, they could hide enemies. Light from one doorway, dim light as if reflected around a corner. Put my head through to reveal a hallway. Light came from one door up.

Tried to be stealthy. Really did. But this body wasn't built for silence, just speed and power. Steps creaked beneath the hardwood floors. Heard a sharp intake of breath from the lit room. "Who's that?"

Froze. Considered. Woman's voice, Spanish accent. Likely friendly. The battle-lust retreated somewhat, letting me gather my thoughts. But it lingered, bubbling, below the surface, never far away. Waiting until I needed it.

"A friend of Addie's," I replied cautiously. And then I walked right in, stealth be damned. YOLO.

The woman watching me suspiciously and fearfully from behind a stove was young, I think. But old-young, like ill use and circumstance had aged her more than time. Her dark hair was drawn up into a tight bun, and when she saw me, she relaxed a little. She wasn't holding a gun or trying to kill me, which was a plus. That's the kinda thing you look for in a friend.

I skirted around the central island/stove. "I'm Kira."

Her face brightened. "Kira. Addie talks much about you."

"It's nice to meet you, Mrs. Bristol," I said, not sure how to address the elephant in the room.

"Ms. Mendez, now," she corrected me, turning back to her pot and giving it a slow, ponderous stir.

"Sorry, Ms. Mendez—"

"—Do not be—"

"—but I'm here because people are coming to kill you. I'm not joking. They could be here any minute."

How about nice and direct? That oughtta work.

I held her gaze, urging her to feel how fucking serious I was. Her face hardened slowly and I knew she believed me. "I have paid them, the *bolillos putos*."

"They're coming anyway."

It hadn't been high on the list of important shit, but I'd been wondering how to convince Addie's mom she was in danger without telling her everything. In this case, I figured going with her guess was a little white lie that'd save Addie some trouble later.

Slowly, as if in a daze, she turned off the stove. "How do you know? Where are the police?"

"I'll explain later," I lied. "Upstairs. Take this and hide." I pulled a long, black-handled kitchen knife from the rack and pressed it into her limp hand. Held it there until her fingers closed around it. "Don't come down until I say."

She didn't move. Her eyes had unfocused, like she was revisiting some awful memory. A small push towards the door got her started moving again, but then she turned around, remembering something.

"What about you?"

"I won't be here." Another lie. "There's a plan." Lie number three.

I tried to project confidence, hoping she wouldn't want details. Again, I'm not Addie, not the best actor ever. But you don't scam as many people as me without picking up some tricks.

In this case, it worked. Ms. Mendez gave me a brave, motherly smile, and then hurried out the kitchen door, holding the knife tightly. I waited until her footsteps receded and then turned my attention back to the knife rack.

I stood there longer than I could spare, wondering if I should take one. If I did, I wouldn't hesitate to use it. I've never killed anyone, and I had no intention of starting today. But if Addie's mom was killed because I hadn't grabbed that fucking knife while I had the chance . . .

My hand shot forward and took one before I could stop myself. Well-polished and thin, with a wood handle. I swung it experimentally.

A last resort. Or so I told myself. In the back of my mind, I knew I'd basically used it already. It's a little scary how easy it is to stop thinking about shit like that.

I snapped out of it when I heard a car pull up outside. No time for philosophical shit. Not now.

I took large strides down the hallway into a living room by the front door. I considered the furniture, alcoves, and doorways, and finally decided to hide behind an overstuffed green couch. I crouched, head bent so it wouldn't show over the top, knees tense and ready to spring. I slowed my breathing and my heartbeat. I wasn't afraid.

I was born for this.

I waited. Nothing. No knock at the door, no footsteps in the yard. Then I heard another car come to a stop outside the house. Doors opened, closed. Then footsteps on the concrete steps.

The door creaked as it opened. I closed my eyes and let the battle-lust settle into my muscles, welcomed it like an old friend.

Senses sharpened. Time slowed.

Footfalls on the hardwood, slowly approaching my position. Three distinct sets. Could hear their shallow breathing.

Arms trembling. Wanted a fight *now*, no waiting. Forced myself to stay hidden. Tactical advantage important. Don't squander. Waited until I saw the tip of the first man's shoe.

Knees straightened. Burst up like a jack-in-the-box. Buried my knife to the hilt in his chest. Didn't bother drawing it out. Let go. He fell forward. Ex-threat now.

Shouts, gasps from other threats. Surprised, off-balance. But they recovered well. Front threat leveled a pistol at my face. Hand shot forward like a striking snake. Slapped the barrel aside as he fired. Bullet whistled past my ear.

Grabbed his arm and pulled, using him as a shield. Other threat fired, but just to scare. Shot didn't come close. Couldn't risk it.

Red vision. Brain calculating positions, movements, outcomes. One enemy down, likely dead. Two threats, one in striking range.

Grabbed him by his collar with my other hand. Lifted him bodily. Then *threw*. Kicked him in the chest as he flew, adding momentum. He crashed into his partner. Rushed forward in his wake. Dove on his splayed body. Pinned his arms beneath my knees. Other threat was beneath him. Arms and gun trapped between their bodies.

Struck the top threat between the eyes. Watched

them rolled back. Other man strained, helpless beneath our combined weight. Spat in my face, glaring hatred at the six-foot blonde who'd taken out his partners. Could see his hate through the red haze, it was so strong.

Smiled at him sweetly. Leaned forward to wrap my hands around his neck. Both thumbs below the Adam's apple and squeezed until his breath was gone.

And my blood sang its joy.

Heard a bang and whipped around. Third clinging to life. Had somehow raised his gun and fired, but the shot'd gone awry. Rolled off the limp men towards him. Shot again, but his whole body was trembling and my roll made me a small target. Another miss.

Easily wrenched the gun from his weakening fingers. Shot point-blank. He tumbled back. Hole in his head. Blood splashed onto face, shirt, couch. Painting me.

Turned back to the man I'd punched unconscious.

Fired again. Hit him just below the left eye. He spasmed a bit before lolling back.

The fire in my blood drained slowly once the threats were gone. Breath by breath, the red mist receded from my vision and I looked at what I'd done with new, saner eyes. At the three corpses that'd once been living and breathing.

And I know what I should've felt. Weak. Drained. Horrified, sick, even just *sad*. Staring at those bodies, I tried to. I tried harder than I'd ever tried anything before.

But I couldn't. The feelings wouldn't come. There was an icy pit in my stomach, an emptiness where my regret should've been.

And the *really* ironic thing? Not feeling that disturbed the shit outta me. I didn't care that I'd killed three men, but I cared that I didn't care. That tickled me somehow, and I started laughing. I didn't feel like laughing, but I did anyway, still holding the gun, still looking like a Pollock done with blood instead of paint.

I heard footsteps from the hallway and whirled, pointing the gun. But it was only Mrs. Mendez, looking horrified at the gore I'd left in my wake, reacting like a normal human would. She flinched away as I faced her.

"You shouldn't've come down," I said roughly. It was all I could think to say. But I lowered the gun. She didn't look any less frightened.

She shook her head. "*Que pasó?*" It was more accusation than question.

The police were coming. Remembering was a cold shock to my system.

"Tell them there were four. They came to rob you. You hid and they quarreled. Three were killed, the fourth escaped." The words came stumbling out. I had to leave. Nobody could know.

Not the cops. And definitely not my friends.

They already think I'm crazy. *Kira the adrenaline junky. Not too bright, just looking for a rush, but good to have around in a fight.* I let them think that because it's better than them knowing the truth. Way better than *Kira the killer.*

I stepped over the first man I'd shot, toward the hallway, toward Mrs. Mendez, who took a small, automatic step back. I couldn't even blame her. What the fuck *was* I?

"Don't tell Addie," I muttered as I passed her, trying not to make it sound like a threat.

As much as I tried, I couldn't quash the spring in my step.

2

THE BASEMENT WAS SO QUIET, WE COULD HEAR every noise from upstairs. Every yell, every shot, every crunch of breaking wood. But even though each new noise brought its own stab of fear, I was grateful they hadn't stopped. As long as the sounds kept up, Dad was still fighting, which meant he was still alive.

I wanted to block them out, but they were my only look at what was happening upstairs. So

I forced myself to listen to the thuds of running boots and shouted, muffled orders until my fingernails were digging into my palms, and the inside of my cheek was bleeding into my mouth. But it was like trying to read a book by smell. All I could do was pray and hope God thought that was enough.

Jason, the son of a bitch who'd got us into this mess, straightened up proudly. He'd been rooting through the boxes that made up our makeshift barricade like something in them could save us. For a second, I felt almost hopeful. Jason has a habit of pulling miracles outta his ass. But it was just a fishing rod. He swished it back and forth, making a snapping sound. And the hope I'd been almost feeling died.

"You gonna whip someone to death with that?" I said, not bothering to hide my scorn.

He just shrugged. "Maybe."

Loud stomping from upstairs. Three or more people were changing position real fast. They'd been getting closer to the basement since the fight began. This barricade was Dad's final, desperate position. One entrance. Easy to defend, but impossible to escape.

My phone said only two minutes'd passed since the shots started. It felt like a lifetime ago.

Jason started pawing through the boxes again and I almost joined him, just to distract myself from the creeping dread. There had to be *something* useful down here. Maybe. Like the handsaw that cut down our Christmas tree every year. But that was flimsy as fuck. I'd be better off throwing the ammo Dad'd left by a sixteen-pack of water bottles.

Someone was coming down the stairs, so fast I didn't even have time to hope it was Dad before he burst into the room. My heart leapt when I saw he was OK. He was sweating, and looking like he usually does before he starts yelling, but he was still moving, still fighting, by the grace of God. He smiled to see me but didn't stop moving until he was safe behind the barricade with us. Only then did I hear the footsteps behind him.

"Should've kicked you out when I had the chance," he grunted, leveling his gun at the stairwell. Two feet appeared on the highest stair we could see.

"Plug your ears," said Dad, and in the time it took him to say that, the feet made it down another three steps and had started growing legs. I had just enough time to get my hands over my ears before Dad's gun went off twice. The feet withdrew hastily, and the steps on the staircase stopped.

Even with the warning, my ears were ringing. Jason was frowning, prodding at his ear. Soft bastard'd probably never held a gun, much less heard one. Dad'd been taking me to the range since I was eight . . . but it hadn't prepared me. Not for this.

"They're good," said Dad. He was wasting no time, already reloading from the ammo-pile. "Good thing I set this last place up, huh? Hell, but I hoped it wouldn't come to this."

"How many are there?" Jason asked. His voice came out louder than it should've.

"Counted five," said Dad.

Five. And I'd thought it'd be three at most. I glared at Jason again, but he didn't notice. He had his thinking-face on, the face he gets before telling me how I'm gonna get screwed over.

"You hit anything?" he asked.

Dad snorted. "Minor injuries. They're all still up. Haven't had much chance to take good shots. They keep flanking me, or else my vision's going in my old age."

Dad always complained about getting old, even though he was just forty-three. Under different circumstances, I'd've teased him about it. Now I might not get the chance. I felt a sudden rush of tenderness, and had to blink away tears before Jason saw.

"Dad—"

"I know," said Dad. He took my hand and squeezed it gently, the same way he'd always done when I was little and having nightmares. Somehow it still comforted me, even though this was more real than any nightmare. "I'm so sorry. I never thought my job'd come home like this. I don't understand how it happened."

I couldn't help it, I cleared my throat meaningfully. This time, Jason noticed and sent me a sharp look. I looked away in embarrassment. He was right, now wasn't the time to play the blame game.

"Actually," Dad said to him, "how *did* you know this was coming?"

I'll never know what Jason would've said, because any possible answer was interrupted by a sudden hail of bullets from the stairwell. They all fell short, though, the staircase's angle made hitting us pretty much impossible. I clapped my hands over my ears as fast as possible, but there was still a persistent ringing when the gunfire stopped.

"Still alive down there?"

The voice was muted somewhat, like I was hearing it through water. But even so, it sounded carefree and jovial, more fit for a day at the zoo than an assassination.

Dad motioned us to plug our ears, then responded with a spray of bullets until he was out. There was no chance he'd hit anything, but the shots sent a clear message, that we had so many bullets we weren't worried about wasting them.

He started reloading again while we stayed braced for the next salvo, Jason still holding the stupid fishing rod. But there were no new shots.

Hesitantly, I took my hands off my ears and listened.

"We did it," said Jason.

I didn't know what he was smoking, but then I heard it too. Police sirens, growing louder and louder . . . and then stopping, one by one. Dad didn't lower his gun one bit.

"They could decide they like it better down here than up there," he said. I was starting to get why Jason'd wanted him here. Still pissed as fuck he was using Dad the same way he uses all my friends, but maybe willing to forgive him. Maybe.

Dad asked me to call the station and see who they'd sent so we could contact them. The signal was shit, but it was worth a shot. I dialed.

"Come out with your hands behind your heads. The building is surrounded." The familiar sound of a police-issue megaphone shook the walls. But if there was a response, we couldn't hear it.

"Wish Addie were here," I said softly, looking at Jason. She would've been perfect to spy upstairs. I'm pretty sure he'd been having the same thought.

"We're listening. Don't do anything rash," said the megaphone.

Finally, someone at the station picked up. Once I'd explained who I was, they patched me right through to Marcus Lowell, the ranking officer. I'd seen Marcus around the station a bunch, and even dated his daughter a couple times. Not that he knew that.

But he was one of the good ones. Knowing he had our backs made me feel safer.

The connection was so bad, it made Marcus sound like he was wrestling a cat in a forest of tinfoil, but through the interference, I could sense his calm.

"*Kkkkkk* hear from *kkkkkk*. *Kkkkkk* to Hector, please?"

"Sure," I said to him, hoping it was understandable on the other end. Then I looked up at Dad. "He wants to talk to you."

"Hold it in place," said Dad, keeping both hands on his gun. So I did, keeping the phone pressed tight against his ear.

"Marcus, you bastard. I was hoping they'd sent you," he said with a smile. "We got five hostiles, all with semi-automatic weapons. What's the deal out there?"

Marcus's response made Dad frown. No idea how he could hear it, since the disturbed-tinfoil-forest noise was loud enough to reach *me*.

"They're lying," he said. "There's three people in here, and we're all safe."

"They said we're hostages?" asked Jason, and Hector nodded once.

The wait stretched on, and my thoughts drifted to Addie and Kira. Especially Kira. Someday I'm gonna date that girl, when I don't think she'll kick my ass for asking. She's literally perfect. Tall, blonde, athletic, and she can punch out anyone who mouths off to her. She's the toughest person I know, but surely that had limits, right? She couldn't fight five grown men with guns. She just *couldn't*. And if she wasn't okay . . . My blood ran cold just thinking it. How could Jason just sit there so calm? Didn't he get it? I knew he was into Addie, wasn't he worried about *her* at all? Did he care she might be dying right now, shot on his orders?

"Tell whoever's outside not to tell the mobsters we know they're lying," said Jason, staring blankly at the barricade. He was in thinking-mode again.

"Or they might decide they need real hostages and come looking for some."

"Hold a sec, Marcus." Dad poked me and I tilted the phone away from his mouth. "What's your plan, then?"

I wanted to make sure Dad understood what a bad idea asking Jason's advice was, but Jason was too quick.

"Send in a team while pretending to negotiate. Hit them fast and hard while they think we bought the lie, nonlethal force if possible, but not a requirement given the circumstances. It'll be over before they have a chance to think of sheltering down here."

For once, Jason's plan *didn't* sound like it was gonna fuck me. That didn't mean it wasn't gonna later, but I had to admit, it *seemed* like it'd work. Dad liked it too, he repeated it right back to Marcus.

"What are your demands?" asked the megaphone a few minutes later. Hector winked at Jason.

We could only hear half the discussion, but

Marcus kept Dad updated and with his help, we could keep track of things. The Mafia wanted to leave with their hostages and set us free later. The cops were testy about the lack of evidence that there *were* hostages, but thanks to Dad's instruction, they didn't press the matter as hard as they would've otherwise. Dad kept his gun pointed at the stairs the whole time. He stayed on the line but only spoke when Marcus asked him a straight question.

"Alright, boys," he said at last. "They're starting the countdown. Eight seconds until the team moves in."

His tongue clicked against his teeth like a ticking clock, one click per second, and he shoved my phone back at me with his cheek. Taking the hint, I hung up and tucked it away.

Four clicks . . . Five . . . On nine, the upstairs got loud again. More shots, more thumps, more splintering wood. That was our living room they were shooting up, and they didn't even care.

After about thirty seconds, gunshots got a

bunch less common. I guess both sides'd settled behind Dad's barricades. It was more stalemate than anything. I had a crazy thought of charging up and rushing them from behind, which I guess is why I wasn't surprised when Dad started tiptoeing towards the stairs.

"Where you going?" I said sharply. But he didn't need to tell me, I knew.

Dad froze at once. He must've known I'd call him out. "Gonna flank them from behind," he said. "End it quick."

"But we're safe down here."

"Son, my friends are up there." Dad said in his disappointed voice. It was soft and low, and partnered with a stern, rebuking stare. "Men and women I work side by side with. Some of them have saved my life. And every second this fight continues is another chance for a bullet to find one of them. I couldn't live with that."

I don't think I've ever stood up to that look. My family's real big on obedience. Listening to Dad's something I just *do*. His house, his word. But I didn't back down. It felt wrong, but letting Dad go would've felt worse.

I *knew*. I knew if he went, I'd never see him again.

"I'll be back in a bit," he said.

Eight long steps took him to the landing. Eight long, powerful footsteps, like a mighty tiger. But I wasn't a kid anymore, hadn't been for years. And I knew what kids never suspect, that my dad wasn't invincible. I pleaded with my eyes, my words, everything. None of it mattered. Dad was too *good* to leave his friends fighting alone when he could help.

If Jason'd helped convince him, maybe he would've listened. Dad'd been listening to him like he'd never listened to me, and Jason could've made up whatever bullshit rationale Dad needed to hear. He does it all the time. But he didn't. Of course he didn't.

What'd *he* care?

His steps were quiet, or maybe it was just that the noise from upstairs drowned them out. Up the stairs he went until I could just see his legs, and then his feet, and then he was gone.

Gone.

Jason's hand was squeezing my shoulder. I think he was trying to be comforting, but I ignored him. I was concentrating fully on the prayer in my mind, which I wasn't speaking out loud because Jason would just laugh. *God, if you never grant another prayer of mine again . . .*

"It's a sound plan," said Jason. "The element of surprise is often the sole determining factor in—"

More shots rang out, a whole bunch. And then I heard the sound I was dreading more than anything else.

Dad's yell.

And my heart tore itself apart.

I think I shouted something. I can't remember, though. All I remember is the weight of my despair crushing me, and then opening my eyes, but I don't remember shutting them. I realized I was standing, which was weird, because I'd been expecting to find myself on the ground. How could I not be when my heart felt so heavy, so sore?

Before I knew what I was doing, I was leaping over the barrier. Dad was in trouble, I needed to—

My shirt caught around my neck and something yanked me back. I fell backwards onto Jason and we toppled onto the stone floor. In that moment, I hated him like I've never hated anyone and I punched at him, scratched, kicked, whatever I could.

"Lemme up!" I growled between breaths. "That was Dad, I know it was, I *heard him*—"

He was saying something too, but I was done listening to him.

"He might need help, I need to help him!"

"They'll kill you too the moment you poke your head out!"

Jason repeated that over and over until it sunk in and my limbs got heavy in tiredness and despair.

Once I'd stopped fighting him, Jason released my shirt and arms. I crawled back into a sitting position (even that was a struggle) and buried my head in my hands. He was right, that asshole. I couldn't go up there, or do anything but sit in my basement while Dad died.

"He might just be hurt," said Jason. "Only about five percent of bullet wounds—"

"Shut up," I suggested. By some miracle, he listened.

I dunno how much longer the shooting went on, and I didn't care. Couldn't even say for sure when it stopped. I sat against the wall staring at my palms from close-up until I realized Jason and Marcus were talking.

"We're clear," I heard Marcus say.

We're clear. We're clean. I wonder if Jason knew how close his old CPC password was to police lingo. That club'd been trouble for me since day one. Screwing me over, time and time again.

And now . . . I took off running, trying to leave

the sickness in my gut behind, and pushed past Marcus, barely even noticing he was there. Jason yelled something, but there was a roaring in my ears that wasn't from noise damage and I didn't listen.

Even through the hot tears blurring my vision I could see how bad my home looked. Burn marks and bullet holes, shattered windows and splintered furniture, and blood in every amount from drops to puddles, like a hurricane had blown through.

I almost convinced myself God had heard me, that by some miracle Dad was fine and that he'd laugh and ask if I'd been worried. And then I saw him, face up in a small pool of blood. The best role model I ever had. The guy who'd bandaged my scrapes and chased away the monsters under the bed and driven me to the range whenever I asked. Dad. Such a short word, but enough to bring seventeen years of memories with it. And the memories dragged tears behind.

It was too late to say "goodbye," or "I'm sorry,"

or even just "I love you." Too late to hear his last words or be the last thing he saw. It'd *been* too late for minutes now.

I was crying freely, and the rest of the house, cops and all, had faded to nothing around me. Whatever pain I thought I'd felt in the basement was nothing to what I felt now. I'd swallowed razors and they'd come to life as they'd passed my chest.

It was the Mafia's fault. It was Jason's fault. It was the CPC's fault. It was my fault. It didn't matter, because whoever's fault it was, it didn't change that Hector Davis, my dad, had died without his wife and kids to help him along to Heaven. He'd died alone.

Just like I was now.

JEEVES

JEEVES HAD TRACKED DOWN MR. JORGENSEN'S previous three personal assistants and interviewed them before accepting the post himself. Jeeves was nothing if not thorough.

Jeeves had listened to their tales of woe, tales that painted a picture of a man gone mad with wealth and power. He had heard the reasons behind all three former employees' decisions to resign. Jeeves was nothing if not prepared.

Jeeves had weighed their testimony carefully, then accepted the job anyway, intending to do his best every day and to not let Mr. Jorgensen's peculiarities phase him. Jeeves was nothing if not proud.

It was shaping up to be another idle day at the Jorgensen estate. Jeeves had hundreds and hundreds of e-mails to answer—all for Mr. Jorgensen, of course, but a man of his importance could hardly be expected to read his own mail. It was Jeeves's job, whenever he had downtime, to reply to the dozens of people trying to contact Mr. Jorgensen, and to never allow them to even suspect that they had interacted with anything but the genuine article. Jeeves was very proud of his "personal touch."

The intercom crackled, and the voice of Mr.

Jorgensen himself echoed through the room. "Coffee, Jeeves!"

Jeeves rose and began to make his way toward the kitchen. Mr. Jorgensen was only one room over, through an elaborate set of double doors, but he rarely—if ever—opened them to give Jeeves as simple an order as coffee. Why do such an inefficient thing when he had a perfectly good intercom system?

Jeeves pressed the SPEAK button. "Yes sir," he said crisply, in the British accent he'd been forced to learn upon landing the job. Mr. Jorgensen was insistent that his personal assistant, alright, *butler*, have a proper English accent. Actually, Jeeves wasn't his birth name either, but it had been made clear to him that if he accepted the job, his name would be Jeeves—and not Brian—from that moment on.

"Jeeves is the only proper name for a butler, and I won't accept any butler who isn't perfectly proper," Mr. Jorgensen had said by way of explanation, leaning back in his armchair. "I used to only look at candidates who were already named Jeeves, but now I think it amuses me far more to have someone give up their name to work for me. Don't you agree, Jeeves?"

Jeeves had nodded politely, but earnestly—a masterpiece of a polite little butler's nod.

The kitchen was relatively close, considering the house's size. It was actually more of a kitchenette, hastily installed to decrease Jeeves's travel time—not for *his* sake, of course, but for the sake of the coffee's temperature. Other staff kept a pot of coffee piping hot by the stove at all times, ready for Jeeves to pour—which he did.

He carried the coffee—black, no sugar—on a small tray back up the stairway, down the hall, into the office, and through the double doors where Mr. Jorgensen sat waiting in his red-paisley-carpeted study, surrounded by papers.

"Your coffee, sir," said Jeeves. He placed it on the coffee table and received a grunt by way of reply.

Back through the double doors to his own room, far more modestly furnished. He was just sitting back down to his work when—

"Sir," said Jeeves into the intercom, "we appear to have a security breach."

One thing was certain—the day was no longer idle.

"Camera eighty-four shows three men advancing on the house through the sculpted hedges. They have disabled the primary alarm, but the silent alert on the security console apprised me of the situation. Shall I notify law enforcement, sir?"

Most security systems would send an automated alert to the police station of choice, but Mr. Jorgensen preferred to decide whether he wanted their assistance on a case-by-case basis . . . just in case he didn't want them around.

The intercom made a confused, staticky sound as Mr. Jorgensen sighed into it. "I suppose. Now, don't disturb me again unless it's important."

Jeeves didn't waste his breath responding, but

instead routed the silent alarm through to the NYPD. Then he returned to sending e-mails while keeping an eye on the cameras.

It quickly became apparent that the intruders were headed for the office. They advanced with skill and caution, easily evading the minimal security details. Jeeves's hand toyed idly with the intercom button, wondering if he should inform Mr. Jorgensen. He made his decision when the three men at last encountered a guard and drew guns.

"Sir, the three intruders are armed and moving towards this location. Furthermore, while police have arrived at the gate, they will not arrive in time to fend the intruders off. I suggest you—"

Before Jeeves could complete his sentence, there was a low rumble, and thick panels of metal folded out from the edges of the double doors, covering the entrance to Mr. Jorgensen's study with an impenetrable barrier.

"—engage the emergency protocols," finished Jeeves.

Metal sheeting dropped from the ceiling to cover the wall around the door, forming a bulwark. Mr. Jorgensen was safe behind two feet of solid steel, which took a great weight off Jeeves's mind. He looked back at the security feed. The guard was on his knees with his hands behind his head, and the three assassins—for what else could they be?—had moved on. They were at the end of the long hall-way now, four doors away.

The voice that emerged from the intercom was tired and fed up. "Deal with this, won't you, Jeeves?"

"Yes sir," said Jeeves without the slightest hes-itation. He reached into his desk's central drawer and retrieved a pair of earplugs, which he screwed firmly into his ears. Then, still sitting, he waited.

Seemingly aware that they had little time before the police arrived, the assassins wasted no time in closing the distance down the hallway. Jeeves watched the door from the outside and the inside simultaneously as it opened.

"Evening," said Jeeves mildly.

The man at the head of the group walked slowly toward him, motioning with his gun. With a resigned sigh, Jeeves raised his arms above his head.

"On the floor," said the man in a thick Italian accent. Jeeves could barely hear him through the earplugs, but obliged him by sliding out of the chair, sinking to his knees, and letting himself fall backwards behind the desk into a prone position. As he did so, the man moved around the desk to keep him in view.

"Where is Jason Jorgensen?" he asked.

Jeeves replied by lashing out with his leg, entangling the intruder's foot with his own. With a sharp pull, he brought the unfortunate assassin down on top of him.

As his opponent fell, he managed to fire, but his aim was wildly off and the bullet buried itself in Jeeves' desk. He winced—that was chestnut. An antique.

His opponent didn't get another shot. Jeeves

grabbed his wrists in an iron grip and twisted. The gun clattered to the ground.

Mr. Jorgensen required his butlers to have mastered at least one martial art.

There was shouting from behind the desk, and the sound of gunfire, a dull roar through Jeeves's earplugs. He rolled over onto his back, which placed his opponent face-down underneath him, and rammed an elbow into the back of his skull. Hard.

One down.

Jeeves picked up the dropped gun and hefted it, getting a feel for its weight. Then he rolled around the side of the desk and returned fire. The shots sailed past the man he'd been aiming for and impacted a security monitor. Sparks flew everywhere and Jeeves ducked back behind the desk, narrowly avoiding the return salvo.

But the attempt had given him valuable intelligence about his enemy's location. Jeeves removed one of the left-hand drawers from the desk. Then, almost crying from the property damage he was causing, he thrust the gun into the hole he'd created and out the other side, aiming carefully. He fired, and the sudden scream told him he'd hit his target. Two down.

Amateurs. That would teach them to hold their position.

There was another cascade of bullets against the desk, but it was reduced in volume. Two actually penetrated all the way through, narrowly missing Jeeves. Needless to say, the priceless antique was beyond salvageable at this point.

In one smooth motion, Jeeves stood, sighted, and fired. The third attacker fell, bleeding from the chest. Three down. Jeeves stepped out from behind what remained of his workstation and gathered their weapons, just in case one was still in good enough shape to fire. Both still clinging to life—depending on how quickly the EMTs arrived, they might actually survive.

Jeeves hit the intercom. "All clear, sir."

Slowly, the metal plates retracted. They folded into each other like a deck of cards being shuffled and slid into the hidden grooves they'd come from, revealing once more the imposing double doors.

They opened to reveal all six feet, two inches of Mr. Jorgensen, almost looking like a third door himself. He stared at the wreckage, then at the bodies, then at Jeeves.

"That's chestnut," he said, looking at the desk. "Antique. Hard to replace."

"I know, sir. Sorry, sir."

Mr. Jorgensen harrumphed loudly and leaned on his ivory-tipped cane. He was a fit man—though pushing sixty—but it amused him to carry a cane. "For effect," he often said.

"Who were they?" he asked, walking over to the closest body—the man Jeeves had knocked unconscious with his elbow.

"That one had an Italian accent, sir," said Jeeves. "More details than that, they did not share."

Mr. Jorgensen knelt by the body and reached

into the man's pockets. He produced a phone, which was password-protected, and a wallet, which he flipped through.

"Mafia," he said at last, tossing the wallet aside. He did not explain how he'd arrived at that conclusion, but Jeeves knew he was correct. Mr. Jorgensen did not make pronouncements he was unsure of.

Mr. Jorgensen stood perfectly still for several seconds. Then a smile spread across his wide face. "Well, well, well," he said. "Looks like the pup's finally teething."

"Sir?" Jeeves was used to vague pronouncements like these, and had learned that a polite "Sir?" was enough to prompt Mr. Jorgensen to expand upon them.

"My son is a weakling, Jeeves," said Mr. Jorgensen quietly. "He inherited my brain, but his mother's heart. He should be *ruling* that pathetic children's gang of his. They should be grateful he deigns to involve them in his schemes."

He squeezed the handle of his cane. "Pranks,"

he continued, spitting the word like a curse. "Acts of schoolyard justice and petty revenge. All unworthy of a boy of his stock. But that's how he spends his time, Jeeves, and it's to his detriment. When I think where he'd be if I hadn't intervened . . . " he shook his head in disgust. "The idiot doesn't even question his good luck sometimes. But he has potential, thanks to my genes and parenting. And, if he realizes it, there is a place in my organization for him. My *true* organization."

He turned to face Jeeves fully, his smile growing wider. Jeeves was given the impression of a bow slowly being stretched beyond its breaking point.

"When his handlers reported he'd gotten in trouble with the Vegas Mafia, I knew he was growing into his role. But this, tonight . . . to have made them angry enough to carry out a hit, he must have finally done something worthy of his surname."

Jeeves thought it was more likely that Jason had hired the assassins himself, but didn't voice that thought aloud.

"But sir, how do we know your son is involved?"

"Because, Jeeves, he's been at war with them for the past few weeks, or so his handlers have reported. Anonymously, last I heard, but I suspect that when I receive an update on the situation, I'll learn that he has finally slipped up."

"Of course, sir. I agree, sir."

"There's only one thing I'd like to know," said Mr. Jorgensen thoughtfully, still turned toward Jeeves but looking *through* rather than *at* him, staring at a bullet hole in the wall. "Did Jason know about the attack in advance? And if so, did he not warn me because he knew it would fail, or because he was hoping it wouldn't?"

Jeeves swallowed. His contract forbade lying, and he would die before he violated his contract. But to give his honest opinion here seemed unwise.

Luckily, he was spared answering. The office door flew open and Jeeves was suddenly looking down the barrels of five SWAT-issue guns. Seeing the defused situation, the team moved cautiously into the room, broken glass and wood crunching beneath their boots.

"Stewart, get the ambulance," said one. "Crowe and Peele, you're on stretcher duty. You alright, Mr. Jorgensen?"

"In the pinnacle of health, no thanks to you," Mr. Jorgensen replied, looking down at him. "What took you boys so damned long?"

ELEVEN

I STILL WENT TO SCHOOL THE NEXT DAY.

Yeah, I had the world's best excuse to skip. We'd seriously discussed it, I and the CPC—minus Z, who wasn't answering his phone. But as far as places we could meet without raising questions went, school was still at the top, and we had lots to discuss.

We'd checked in by phone last night, just to make sure everyone'd made it. I won't lie, I almost fainted with relief when I heard Addie's voice. Might've cried a bit too, but don't tell anyone. We were all too relieved and tired and shaken to debrief each other, though—we just wanted to hear each other's voices. Four hits in one night. It was a miracle only one person had died.

Of course, that was one too many. I should've saved *everyone*.

People kept asking if I was OK. News'd traveled faster than I'd predicted, and it seemed like the whole school knew what'd happened—or at least some version of it. I waved them off as best I could. I just wanted some time to wrestle with my thoughts—what I'd done, who I'd failed.

Class passed in a haze of whispers and stares. I *tried* to pay attention, but I kept drifting out of focus, sinking back into my thoughts until I was jarred awake by someone saying my name or looking directly at me. The teachers left me alone, mostly. They understood. Or thought they did.

Lunch period couldn't come soon enough. When the bell snapped me out of my self-reflection, I practically bolted to Room 142 (where we'd arranged to meet that day—we were working on getting Room 206 back, but no luck so far). I was first, for once, and I was grateful to just sit down at the table alone, without even a goldfish for company. I was even more grateful that Addie arrived next.

I heard footsteps on the linoleum and I opened my eyes and turned around just in time to feel her arms around me, *squeezing*. I held her moment by moment, letting the emotional warmth of our contact seep through my skin and into my bones. She settled against me, relaxing her grip only after my ribs ached from the pressure—and even then, only slightly.

"You let me hear you," I said at last.

"What makes you say that?"

"First, you're you. Second, I didn't hear the door. Or your first three steps into the room."

"Fine, I admit it," she sighed. "I didn't feel like sneaking up on you, so I helped you notice me."

"Like I need help," I muttered, and she giggled into my shoulder.

"About fucking *time*."

Kira was standing in the doorway with an *incredibly* satisfied smirk.

"Huh?" I said, looking up. "No. We aren't— we're just happy we—"

I took a quick step backwards to hammer the point home, because obviously, my mouth needed some help.

"Don't be shy about it," said Addie, matching my stride to maintain our closeness. "Kira doesn't care."

"But—"

She kissed me.

For a few blissful seconds, the horrors of the previous day retreated from my mind. There was only Addie, and me, and her lips on mine.

And then, for the second time that minute, Kira ruined everything—this time with loud whooping. We broke apart and glared at her.

"That's enough for now, kids," she said, winking. "You proved me right, that's all I need. I came here for an important meeting, not front-row seats to Jason and Addie's PDA Spectacular."

As much as I wanted to ignore her and keep exploring my newfound . . . whatever-it-was with Addie, she *did* have a point. We had *lots* to discuss, and one lunch period to discuss it in. We pushed some desks together and took seats. Addie and I sat next to each other, reveling in each other's closeness.

By unspoken agreement, we decided to start without Z. None of us'd seen him in class, and when we asked some of his many friends, they hadn't either. Honestly, we couldn't blame him for skipping, so we gave him two more minutes and then moved ahead with Item One—swapping stories.

"So, uh . . . what happened?"

"Nothing too interesting," said Addie. "It all went like you'd predicted. The mob showed up and I distracted them until backup could arrive."

Kira raised her eyebrows. "Distracted?"

"We talked about gardening," said Addie, completely straight-faced. "Tomatoes, mostly."

I stared at her, trying to figure out whether she was telling the truth. She shrugged cheekily back.

"What about you?" she asked Kira, who was also looking skeptical.

"Same," said Kira. "You gave me a plan. Hit stuff, chase 'em off. When Z said the schedule'd been moved up, I double-timed it. Made it there first, then . . . hit stuff until they were chased off. Nice plan, by the way."

"Thanks," I said. "You, uh . . . wow."

In the initial panicked rush, it'd seemed perfectly logical to send a teenager to drive off an unknown number of professional killers with nothing but her bare hands. Now, it seemed like the stupidest plan I'd ever made . . . except apparently, it'd *worked*. It was a miracle she hadn't been hurt, or worse.

"What, you didn't have faith in me?" Kira chuckled, cracking her knuckles.

"Yeah," said Addie, turning her chair around to face me. "A little more faith."

But once her face was out of Kira's sightline, she

gave me a warning look. Before I'd figured out a way to ask her what *that* meant, she'd turned back around, entirely normal.

I recognized it, though—it was Addie's *we-need-to-talk* look.

"I mean, I figured you'd surprise someone and wrestle him into submission or something," I said, trying to pretend everything was normal. "Maybe two. But Kira, there were *five* assassins at Z's place. You didn't—"

"Oh, nah," said Kira. "There was three. It wasn't too hard."

Well, that made *slightly* more sense. But three men with guns still should've been at least two too many. "How'd it go down?"

"Hold that thought," said Addie suddenly. "Jason. Five men at Z's? You've talked to him? Why didn't you tell me?"

Shit.

This wasn't how I wanted to admit I'd stayed at Z's, but I could hardly lie—the deception would last about as long as it took Z to start talking to us again. Better to clarify matters on my terms . . . and with my own slant.

"I decided Z's family needed me more than mine did," I said carefully. "Lucas is paranoid, and his security's more than enough to handle any threat the Mafia could pose, especially with a warning. So I helped at Z's house instead."

They took it better than Z had, at least. Kira was giving me a frosty look, but family meant a lot to her in general. Addie's expression was unreadable, and I wondered if she'd noticed I hadn't explicitly said I'd warned anyone.

But neither of them called me on it.

"It was the right call," I said. "They needed my planning skills at Z's, and the three men dispatched to my house were taken into custody with no casualties."

"Good," said Kira.

And it was, I suppose. As big an asshole as Lucas is, I don't actually want him dead—just *gone*. If that makes sense. But denied that, scaring him a little was acceptable. Even with *his* security, a team of gunmen must've been a *little* disconcerting, right?

"I'm more worried about the mob," I said, deftly changing the subject. "They'll be angry. The sooner we can get people guarding our houses, the better. Don't worry about the cost."

I didn't know where I'd find the money, but I'd *beg* Lucas if I had to. I'd stop at nothing to keep us safe. That I'd lost someone was unacceptable, and I *would* do better.

"Are you sure?" asked Addie. "The mob isn't—"

The classroom door opened. Addie cut herself off mid-sentence before the knob was fully turned. Some mistakes, you only make once.

But it wasn't a teacher this time.

It was Z. A more disheveled Z than the world usually saw, but Z nonetheless.

He stepped into the room, glancing furtively about with bloodshot eyes, dressed in the same gray t-shirt and black denim as yesterday. His hair was missing its usual luster, which was worrisome all by itself. Had he slept at all?

"Hi guys," he said roughly, a little scratchily. "Glad you're all OK."

"Same," said Addie. "That is, are you?"

"Knew you would be," Z continued, ignoring her. "That was the *plan*, after all. And we all know how Jason's *plans* go—they work. Perfectly. Sure, Z gets screwed, but whatever . . . right?"

He turned his head to look right at me as he spoke, and I looked away. I couldn't help it— the brimstone in his stare was too raw to handle. Random chance'd targeted Z so many times over the course of our partnership, I was pretty sure they were officially nemeses. If I were him, I'd probably suspect I was doing it on purpose too.

But I wouldn't *really* believe that. And he didn't either.

"I guess it was only a matter of time," said Z, still looking at me. Was that *dried blood* on his hands? "How many times *could* I get screwed, and how badly? You're smart, Jason, you can figure this one out."

"Z," I said as evenly as I could. "I'm so sor—"

"One time too many, and pretty *fucking* badly," said Z venomously. "That's the answer. But it was all part of the plan, of course. That right?"

"Nobody was supposed to—"

"Bull*shit* nobody was supposed to die!" snapped Z. "You put Dad in that house, Jason. You *told* him to stay. Mom's fine. Val's fine. Axel's fine."

I could've pointed out that Hector'd made his choice before I even started talking, but something in Z's expression told me that was a bad idea.

"I wondered why you stayed," said Z, "in the basement, in danger. You had no reason to be there. It didn't make sense. Not until I thought a bit, anyway. Remembered what we'd been doing for a month, now. And realized you *had* to be there to make sure everything went perfectly."

His mouth twisted, like he was trying to smile but his facial muscles were on strike. "Take down the mob, ain't that right, Jason? Use the police as a weapon, ain't that *right*, Jason?"

My mouth went dry as I connected the dots. That was so *not* what I'd intended, but I knew it made too much sense for Z to stop believing it. And even worse, it was a *good plan*—Hell, I probably *would've* tried it, if I were a total fucking *sociopath*.

"That's not what I wanted," I said. I knew it wouldn't be enough as I said it, but what could I say beyond a denial?

"Bullshit," said Z again. "The mob killed a cop. And now, there's gonna be a crackdown like New York never saw before. A goddamned firestorm like there would never've been if it'd been someone else. The cops'll want blood."

"Jason wouldn't do that," said Kira adamantly.

"Shut up, Kira," said Z, not even bothering to look at her. "Course he would. He's an asshole."

I flushed with anger and bit down on my tongue, hard, before I could give in to the temptation to raise my voice.

"Jason Jorgensen," Z pronounced, just to make sure I got the message. "You're an asshole. You don't give a shit about anyone but your own towering ego. You use people until they're all used up. I ain't used up just yet, but I *am* sick of it. And the way you think you're better than us, I'm sick of that too. Don't try and lie, it's all over your rat face."

"Take a deep breath," I said around the pain in my tongue. "Don't say anything you'll regret."

"Regret this? Nah, I'm taking pictures for my memories. I'm done with you and your fucked-up club. That's all I came here to say."

With that, Z turned on his heel and strode back towards the door.

"Z . . . " said Addie softly.

He stopped. He almost turned back, I could see it. With just one word, Addie'd planted a seed of doubt.

But it wasn't enough. "Don't think this is like Vegas," he said, still facing the door. "I'm not getting roped back in. So don't try it—you'll just piss me off."

The door slammed behind him, leaving stunned silence behind.

Kira whistled.

"Fuck," I said, which I thought summed things up pretty well. I sank back into the chair and closed my eyes, gathering my thoughts. Lucas always told me if you don't have your thoughts in order, you have nothing. Even if you have nothing else, you need your thoughts to acquire *something*—in his case, usually money.

"So that happened," said Kira. "Guess you really pissed him off."

"Yeah." Maybe I should've gone after him, but I don't think I could've talked him down. He was angrier than I'd ever seen him . . . and for good reason.

I'd survived all my friends abandoning me at once. Surely, I could survive just one.

Someone slipped a small hand into mine and

gave it a reassuring squeeze. Addie. I leaned against her, and she curled herself under my arm and rested her head on my neck.

"We're gonna leave the Mafia alone for the foreseeable future," I said, drawing strength from the space between our hands, from the closeness of our bodies. "The CPC was three big fish in a small pond before it was four in a big one. We can return to our old pond for now. Nothing wrong with that."

Nothing but the bodies we'd left behind.

We sat there a little longer, saying nothing. Then Kira pulled out her phone and started texting, so I figured it was safe to slide my head closer to Addie's ear and whisper, "What was that look earlier?"

She tilted her head to respond. "You know what Kira said happened at my house?"

I nodded once, as imperceptibly as I could.

"She *lied.*"